WILD DOG REVENGE

A KENYA KANGA MYSTERY

VICTORIA TAIT

KANGA
PRESS

Dedication
To my loyal and wonderful ARC Team
particularly Candy Lawless, Karen Siddall, Anne Kovic,
Jackie Houchin, Kathryn Sauro
and Kathleen Costa.

You have been like Aunts to me, encouraging my writing but at the same time pointing out errors, typos etc.

Thank you

STYLE & KISWAHILI GLOSSARY

The main character, Mama Rose, has a British upbringing and she uses British phrases.

Kiswahili words are used to add to the richness and authenticity of the setting and characters, and most are linked to this Glossary.

- *Asante Thank you*
- *Ayah* Nanny
- *Bob* Slang for Kenyan shilling, currency of Kenya
- *Boda Boda* Motorbike used as a taxi
- *Bwana* Sir, a term of respect used for an older man

- *Chai* Tea consisting of bags or leaves boiled in a mixture of $2/3^{rd}$ water and $1/3^{rd}$ milk
- *Habari* Greeting used like hello but meaning 'What news?'
- *Hapana* No
- *Kikapu* Straw or reed woven basket
- *Kikoi* Brightly coloured cotton material, garment or sarong
- *Mpesa* Mobile money sent from one phone account to another
- *Mzungu* European/White person
- *Pesa* Money
- *Pole* Sorry
- *Pole Pole* Slowly (slowly)
- *Shamba* Farm, garden or area of cultivated land
- *Simama* Stop
- *Syce* A groom/someone who looks after horses
- *Tusker & Whitecap* Brands of beer brewed by East African Breweries

CHAPTER ONE

Rose Hardie lifted her veterinary bag into the back of her battered, red Land Rover Defender. In her mid-sixties, she was tall and lanky and wore a pair of cotton trousers which stopped just above her bony ankles. She gasped as she let go of the bag's leather handles and wiggled her arthritic fingers.

Rose heard her phone ring and patted her pockets. The sound grew louder, and she turned her head of short, frizzy white hair towards her thatched cottage.

Kipto, her house girl, approached carrying Rose's green tote bag and holding a phone at arm's length. Kipto's dark skin was like well-worn leather with deep lines folded into it, and grooves running under her cheeks, creating small pouches of skin.

Rose took the phone and answered it without checking the display. "Habari."

"Habari, Mama Rose." The caller was Dr Emma, who was technically her boss. Rose's full title was 'Veterinary Paraprofessional' and she helped Dr Emma, a fully qualified vet, perform operations in her small pharmacy.

Rose's patients were usually larger animals which could not be brought to the pharmacy or were located outside her hometown of Nanyuki, on Kenya's Laikipia plateau.

In the local community, she was known as 'Mama Rose' and she'd tended to the needs and ailments of animals and wildlife for over forty years.

"I have the rabies vaccine you requested," said Dr Emma.

"Great, shall I pick it up from your pharmacy?"

"No, I have it with me at the new premises."

Rose turned left out of her gate and was greeted by a spectacular view of Mount Kenya, in whose shadow Nanyuki was located. The small market town was three hours drive north of Nairobi, Kenya's capital, and had been established over a hundred years before by European settlers and farmers.

She drove towards the town centre but turned off the main highway, onto a track leading to the Cottage Hospital, and swung through a pair of open metal gates.

Dr Emma's white Probox car was parked in front of a single-storey building which was constructed of concrete blocks with a red-tiled roof.

As Rose turned off the ignition, Dr Emma emerged from the building and removed a small, blue plastic cool box from her car. Dr Emma had a petite figure but everything else about her was enormous: her full afro-style hair, round yellow-framed glasses and wide, inviting smile.

"Here you are. One vial of rabies vaccine for a horse," declared Dr Emma, handing over the cool box.

"Asante." Rose turned her head as she heard another vehicle enter the compound.

Thabiti parked and jumped out of a white Land Cruiser. He was a neat African man in his early twenties with short hair, and a trim beard and moustache encircling his mouth. He wore a pair of blue chino shorts and a crisp white t-shirt.

"Habari, Mama Rose, Dr Emma."

"Excellent," exclaimed Dr Emma, rubbing her hands together. "Do you have the plans?"

Thabiti leaned into his car and extracted a roll of papers.

"Would you like to look at the changes we're considering for this building?" Dr Emma asked Rose.

Thabiti flattened the drawings on the bonnet of his car and Rose peered down at them. "I'm afraid I can't make out all the details. I've left my glasses in the car."

Dr Emma turned to Thabiti. "You explain. I get carried away."

Thabiti pointed to the left side of the plan and explained, "This is the new veterinary practice. The main door will lead into a waiting room and reception. This room," he tapped the paper, "will be partitioned into two consulting rooms, and the adjacent room converted to a new operating theatre."

"And we're building a small extension on the side from which to sell dog food, cat litter and other supplies." Dr Emma beamed proudly.

Rose tilted her head. "It looks like an ambitious project. But won't you need more staff for the extra consultation room, reception and shop?"

Dr Emma shook her head and her hair bobbed from side to side. "Just a receptionist, who I'd also like to train up to be a veterinary nurse. Then I won't have to bother you whenever I need assistance with an operation. And I thought you'd find the extra consulting room useful for say, administering rabies vaccinations to local dogs. And I can invite vets from Nairobi to run specialist clinics."

Thabiti returned to the plans. "And the girls are doing some work on the right-hand section of the building. They're extending the kitchen out to the side, adding new double doors for the entrance, and we're trying to decide what form of canopy or structure to build at the front, or side, to provide shade for the cafe customers."

Rose looked up and surveyed the building. "And are you overseeing the work, Thabiti?" she asked.

"Yes," replied Dr Emma

"Not sure," mumbled Thabiti.

"Please," urged Dr Emma. "Your input in the planning stage has been invaluable, and you know what your sister and her friends want to achieve. Besides, if you are serious about property investment, you'll need to learn to deal with builders and contractors."

Thabiti bit his lip and kicked at a stone on the ground.

Rose's throat tightened as she watched Thabiti. She'd known his mother, Aisha, at school, but they had drifted apart in adulthood. When she discovered Aisha had moved to Nanyuki earlier in the year, with Thabiti and his sister Pearl, she had hoped to rekindle their friendship but, tragically, Aisha had been killed.

Thabiti had persuaded Rose to help him investigate her murder when it appeared the police's hands were tied. He was an anxious young man who disliked groups of people, especially strangers. But he'd developed friendships whilst living in Nanyuki, and Rose had watched his confidence grow.

She laid a hand on his arm and reassured him, "I think it would be both challenging and rewarding to manage the work on this building. And you can discuss anything you're uncertain about with Dr Emma or Marina, Chloe or Pearl."

Thabiti lifted his head and smiled weakly at Rose. "OK. I'll give it a go."

Dr Emma clapped her hands. "Let's have another look inside."

Rose left Dr Emma and Thabiti to discuss their plans for the property and climbed back into her Land Rover.

CHAPTER TWO

R ose drove through the small but bustling town of Timau and continued north. The road climbed as it wound through the foothills of Mount Kenya and some of the most productive farming land in the world.

The North Kenya Polo Club was located at over 8,000 feet above sea level, with Mount Kenya towering above it to the east and the bush country of northern Kenya falling away to the west.

She turned off a dirt track and stopped before a black, metal five-bar gate from which hung a wooden sign with 'North Kenya Polo Club' carved into it. Having closed the gate behind her, Rose took a track on her right, which led to the polo club stables.

African grooms, known as syces, were lazing around on the grass or sitting on circular wooden wedges cut from tree trunks. A few held the ropes of grazing horses, whilst others cradled plastic cups, which she presumed contained chai.

One syce stood and spoke into his mobile phone. As he walked across to the row of clapboard wooden stables, he nodded at Rose and said, "Jasper here soon."

He disappeared into a stable carrying a head collar, and re-appeared tugging on a lead rope to persuade a palomino coloured horse to follow him. Rose approached the horse and stroked its neck of creamy-golden hair. She ran her hand down the back of both its front legs but didn't find any heat, swelling or other sign of injury.

"I suspect it might be a back leg," a powerful male voice declared, "but I can't find any heat or swelling there either."

Rose straightened up and turned to face Jasper Armitage, the owner of the horse. He was in his late twenties and would be described by her younger female friends as ruggedly handsome. His dark hair was slightly too long and his chin bore a splattering of stubble. He had a stocky but athletic build and was considered one of Kenya's top polo players.

"Can we find a flat area of ground to trot him on?" asked Rose. "Is he very sore?"

"He's intermittently lame," Jasper said, as he turned and walked away. "I think it best if we trot him up on the polo pitch."

The syce pulled at the lead rope and the horse turned sharply, and walked unevenly for several steps. Rose heard a vehicle drive past on the far side of the stables heading towards the polo club.

She followed the syce and horse along a well-worn track, between conifer trees, and emerged on the recently mown polo pitch where she joined Jasper. The syce walked the horse past them and then started to run, pulling at the lead rope. But the horse refused to trot, so Jasper ran behind him, waving his arms.

Rose couldn't detect anything wrong. The horse slowed to a walk and the syce turned him tightly and trotted him back towards her. This time the horse's steps were clearly uneven.

Rose carefully approached the horse's hindquarters and ran a hand down both his back legs. As she touched the area below the bony hock joint, the horse flinched, and the area felt slightly warmer.

She straightened up and asked Jasper, "Have you turned him in any tight circles recently?"

Jasper scratched his stubbly chin. "I've done nothing more than stick and ball practice with him since he arrived from Nairobi. But there was a kerfuffle in one of the paddocks yesterday when a pack of wild dogs ran across and scattered the horses. The pack's taken up residence in an old aardvark hole at the edge of the wood, beside the polo pitch. The fields are small, so Trigger could have turned sharply and twisted something. Do you think it's serious?"

Rose ran her hand down the leg again. "It could be, if he's injured his suspensory ligament. I think the damage is high up, in the joint, so it's difficult to tell. I'm sorry, I know he's one of your best polo ponies."

Jasper lowered his head and replied, "He is, along with my chestnut mare, Boadicea. And if he's going to be out for the rest of the season, I'll have to find a replacement. Brian Ellison has been selling some of his polo ponies as he's working away a lot and is concentrating on educating his young horses."

They both looked up and watched two men walk towards them across the polo pitch.

"Is that Dickie?" asked Rose. Dickie Chambers was chairman of the North Kenya Polo Club. He had also been a friend of her late husband's and had given an amusing and moving eulogy at Craig's memorial service two months earlier.

"Yes," replied Jasper. "And I think he's with Yaro Macharia. I wonder if they've come to inspect the wild dog den and decide whether it's safe to hold this weekend's tournament. I'd better join them."

Rose and the syce returned to the stable area where Rose injected Trigger with an anti-inflammatory drug.

"You'll need to cool the right hock twice a day, preferably with a hose pipe, but if you're short of water, spend ten minutes squeezing a sponge of cold water over the area," she instructed the syce.

As she patted the horse's neck, she heard Dickie's voice, so she wandered back towards the polo pitch.

Dickie greeted her, "Hello, Rose. Jasper tells me one of his best horses is out of action this weekend, and probably for next week's tournament as well."

"I'm afraid so. But let's see if he improves. Is everything ready for Saturday?"

Dickie's expression was glum. "It looks like we may have to move to Timau."

"But I didn't think the pitches were ready," remarked Rose.

"The main pitch isn't, but I think we can use No. 2 pitch. My main concern is that the wild dogs have settled here to have their pups, which means we'll have to use Timau for the tournament the following weekend as well."

Jasper looked across to the edge of the conifer wood and commented, "I agree, they look content in their new home."

Rose followed his gaze as two black muzzles protruded from a large hole and sniffed the air. Four adult African wild dogs emerged from their den and took several paces towards her.

"The local village won't like this," remarked Yaro Macharia, standing erect.

Yaro had been a respectable polo player, but he'd retired to run his family's mobile phone business. He pushed his black-rimmed glasses back onto his nose and pinched his lips across his gleaming white teeth.

"Nor will the farmers. Wild dogs can cause considerable damage," added Dickie Chambers. "But they are an endangered species, and I can't see how we can play with their den right beside the pitch."

Jasper placed his hands on his hips. "And they're upsetting the horses, and probably caused Trigger's injury."

Dickie tapped the tips of his fingers together. "I don't think we have a choice. We'll have to move this weekend's tournament to Timau, and hope that we can repair the pitch in time for the following weekend's Mugs Mug polo tournament."

CHAPTER THREE

R ose's second appointment of the day was at the Timau Polo Grounds, which would now host the next two weekends' polo tournaments. A farmer had donated an unproductive area of land on which the polo club had created two polo pitches.

The main pitch, which was located below a recently constructed single-storey brick clubhouse, had been sown with a slow-growing mixture of grasses, and Rose knew it wasn't ready to be played on.

As she drove alongside No. 2 pitch, she noted it was covered in several inches of grass which would need to be cut short and the pitch marked out with white lines in readiness for the weekend's matches.

Rose drove around the far end of the main pitch and turned towards the polo club stables. Unlike the ramshackle wooden ones at the North Kenya Polo Club, these consisted of rows of metal framed stables under a large corrugated-metal roof.

As she carried the blue plastic cool box, containing the rabies vaccine, a long-legged girl in her late teens greeted her.

"Hi, I'm Sophia Gilbert. Have you come to vaccinate Red?"

Sophia was wearing the same red jodhpurs she had worn in Dormans coffee shop a month earlier, when Rose had seen her with another young polo player, Otto Wakeman.

Although the two had not been introduced, Sophia had bought some of Rose's herbal mixes for her horses. Rose created these natural remedies from flowers and herbs which she grew in her shamba and sold to supplement her veterinary income.

"Yes, I have the rabies vaccine."

Most of the stables were empty but the first six had rugs thrown across the metal partition walls. A syce lounged against the wall of a small concrete storeroom and sucked on a piece of straw, as he watched the two women approach.

"Mama Rose," he declared in a flat tone. His stained and faded yellow t-shirt hung loosely on his thin frame and he revealed several missing front teeth when he sneered disparagingly at Sophia.

Rose stopped and stood directly in front of the man. "Gathi, I see someone has taken pity and employed you. But I don't want any trouble this weekend, or at next week's Mugs Mug tournament. Stay off the drink and keep those light fingers of yours to yourself. Where are you staying?"

Gathi jerked his head towards the doorway beside which he lounged. Rose stepped through into the concrete store and noted a compact room with feed bins and buckets along one wall and bridles hanging above them.

On the opposite side, saddles straddled a horizontal pole, and above this was a wooden platform, with an array of blankets and a thin blue mattress.

Rose returned to Gathi and instructed, "Good. But stay away from the bars in Timau."

As Rose and Sophia walked between two rows of stables, Sophia remarked, "That's Felix Kamau's syce. He gives me the creeps. He's been sent here early with Felix's polo ponies."

They stopped beside four occupied stables at the bottom of the row. The stables' metal frames had been neatly covered with used horse-feed bags, which had been sewn together to create dividing screens. Two narrow wooden poles spanned the entrance of each stable to prevent the horses from escaping.

Sophia drew the top pole back on the far stable and lowered one end to the ground. As she stepped over it, she said, "This is Red. Dad bought him from Brian Ellison and he came up from Nairobi with Felix's ponies. Isn't he gorgeous?"

The horse gently butted his golden-orange head against Sophia. He was an unusual strawberry-roan colour, with a cream-coloured body scattered with flecks of orange, and his flowing mane and tail were golden-orange.

Sophia ran her hand through his mane. "It's such a shame I have to cut all this off, but I don't want to risk getting my reins or polo stick caught up in it."

Rose prepared the vaccine and injected Red.

Sophia asked, "Can I ride him this weekend?"

Rose stroked Red's neck and replied, "As long as he doesn't have any adverse reactions. You can lead him out or take him for a short hack this afternoon, and then some gentle stick and ball practice tomorrow."

Sophia's eyes glowed. "I'm so looking forward to trying him out, but I think he might be too good for me." She bit her lip as she stroked Red's head. She gave him a titbit from her pocket and continued, "Felix is arriving later and he said he'd give me a polo lesson tomorrow. But I'll make sure we don't do too much."

As Sophia replaced the pole on the front of the stable, Rose enquired, "I thought you were building stables for your polo ponies on Wild Dog Estate."

"We are, but they're not ready yet. The builders finished the guest cottage, where I'm staying, but there's been an issue with the steel frame for the main house. It's delayed the project, which has annoyed Dad." Sophia wrapped her arms around her body.

"But you're being looked after whilst you're here?" Rose pressed.

Sophia looked up at Rose and her cheeks were flushed. "Oh, yes. Otto and Rufus have been very friendly. They've shown me around and introduced me to some of the other members of the North Kenya Polo Club."

Rose left Sophia tending to her horses. There was no sign of Gathi. Her phone pinged and as she looked at it, her stomach rumbled. She noted it was one o'clock. Where had the morning gone?

The ping informed her of an M-Pesa payment, and she smiled as she read the notification. Jasper Armitage had sent her money for this morning's consultation. Such prompt payment was rare, and she felt unusually extravagant.

An image of the Bushman's Restaurant's cheese and spinach soufflé popped into her mind. Still smiling, she drove back to Nanyuki.

CHAPTER FOUR

Rose entered the Bushman's Restaurant through the bottom gate from the car park. A gravel path led to a row of small shops, but she crossed the garden to an outdoor seating area, beside the single-storey restaurant.

"Rose," called a female voice.

She spotted her young friend Chloe, who stood up and secured her large, round sunglasses in her long, blonde hair. Chloe had met Rose's daughter, Heather, in London at the beginning of the year and when Heather heard that Chloe and her husband Dan were moving to Nanyuki, she'd given her Rose's contact details.

Chloe had not found it easy to settle into life in Nanyuki, especially as her ex-British army husband was away most of the time, working for a security company in northern Kenya.

"Come and join us," invited Chloe.

Rose weaved between tables but stopped when she realised Chloe was not with Thabiti and his sister Pearl, as she had expected. A thickset, muscular man stood up and pulled out a chair for her.

Feeling the colour rise in her cheeks, Rose sat down.

"It's good to meet you," declared the man. Rose recognised a Scottish lilt to his voice. He wore a blue cotton shirt with the sleeves rolled up. When he stretched out his arm to shake Rose's hand, she noticed a tattoo partially hidden by his sleeve.

Chloe introduced her companions. "This is Alasdair and Dorothy Sayers, who've just arrived from the UK. Alasdair served with Dan in the army."

Rose wrinkled her brow and asked, "Alasdair, did you also serve with Chris Hardie?"

Alasdair leaned forward and replied, "Please call me Al, and yes, Chris was with us in Afghanistan."

Chloe's hand shot to her mouth. "Of course. Chris is Rose's son."

Al sat up and tilted his head to one side. Holding steady eye contact with Rose, he remarked, "Then this really is a pleasure."

A waiter approached and handed Rose a menu. She looked enquiringly around the table.

"We've just ordered," disclosed Chloe.

"I'll make sure your meal is served at the same time as your friends," confirmed the waiter.

Rose looked up at him. "Thank you, Geoff, or is it Geoffrey today?" She raised an eyebrow.

He smiled ruefully but did not reply.

Rose ordered. "I'd like a lime juice, with soda water, and a cheese and spinach soufflé with a small side salad."

"Very good," responded the waiter as he picked up the menu.

Rose looked across the table at Al's wife. Her head of shoulder-length, mousy-brown hair was bowed, and she appeared considerably younger than her husband. She jumped when Rose asked, "So, Dorothy, how are you finding Kenya?"

Dorothy's timid voice replied, "I've never been anywhere like this." She raised her head and glanced briefly at Rose. "Do you mind calling me Dotty? Everyone else does."

"So what do you think?" pressed Rose.

Al replied, "Dotty's never been out of the UK before so this is quite an adventure, isn't it my dear?"

Dotty pressed her lips together and nodded.

Chloe asked a little too brightly, "So, Rose, have you had a busy morning?"

Rose sat back as her muscles relaxed. "I have, actually. I've been attending to polo ponies which have arrived for a tournament this weekend."

Chloe leaned forward. "A polo tournament. Where's it being held?"

"It looks like they're moving it to Timau, to the new polo ground, as a pack of wild dogs have taken up residence next to the usual polo pitch."

Dotty placed her arms on the table and looked up. She asked, "African wild dogs?"

"Yes," replied Rose, "although some people refer to them as painted dogs or wolves."

Dotty's eyes were wide. "They're really rare. Do you think we could see them?"

Rose shrugged her shoulders. "I don't see why not."

Al leaned towards Dotty and put a hand on her shoulder. "Now, now. We don't want to bother Rose. She's clearly a busy and important lady."

Rose nearly chocked on the lime and soda which the waiter had placed in front of her. "I'm not at all important, and if I can't take you, I'm sure Thabiti would. In fact, it would be a fantastic photo opportunity for him."

Chloe nodded her head enthusiastically. "I'll talk to him and arrange a visit." She looked at Al and suggested, "Perhaps I can take Dotty and let you and Dan have some time together?"

Al tugged his bottom lip and looked at Dotty. "Perhaps. And when did you say Dan is back?"

Chloe twisted her wedding ring. "He had hoped to be here this afternoon, but it's more likely to be Saturday evening now."

She swallowed. "So perhaps we can visit the polo on Saturday? Experience a little of Kenyan expat life." She glanced round the table.

Dotty smiled. "I'd like that."

CHAPTER FIVE

On Saturday afternoon, Rose joined her friend Poppy Chambers at the Timau Polo Grounds. Poppy was Dickie Chambers' wife, and they had built a house on the adjacent Wild Dog Estate. She had invited Rose to stay overnight.

There were no stands on No. 2 pitch, but several tents had been erected to shade spectators as they watched the polo from rows of white plastic chairs and wooden benches.

A new match was about to begin, and two teams of four players rode onto the pitch. They lined up in front of the tent where Rose and Poppy were sitting.

Dickie strode up to a microphone, positioned on a small table at the front of the tent, and introduced the team members, who wore either blue or red bibs.

The last horse on the blue team refused to stand still and the rider kept turning him in circles. Although his lovely golden-orange mane had been cut off, Rose still recognised the cream body, with flecks of orange, of Red, Sophia Gilbert's new polo pony.

"And the fourth member of the blue team is Sophia Gilbert," announced Dickie.

"Come on, Soph," a man's voice uttered behind Rose.

She turned around and came face-to-face with a clean shaven European man wearing a panama straw hat. She asked, "Is that your daughter?"

The man removed his hat and ran his hand through his spiky white hair. "Yes, and this is her first major competition. She's hoping to get picked for a team to play in next weekend's Mugs Mug tournament."

"That's a lovely horse she's riding," remarked Rose.

"He's new, and a bit of a handful. Soph said having some lessons with Felix Kamau has helped her control him."

Dickie returned to his seat next to his wife and remarked, "I hope Felix controls himself today. I've had to reprimand him on several occasions for overly aggressive play, and bad language."

A whistle blew and the players lined up, facing each other. The mounted umpire, wearing a black and white vertically striped shirt, threw a white ball between the teams and play commenced.

Rose heard a stick strike the ball and it shot towards the left-hand goal, followed by the players riding at high speed. Sophia hung back, but her horse was agitated and started leaping about. She trotted steadily towards the action.

Suddenly, the ball raced across the green turf towards the right-hand goal and passed Sophia. She turned her horse expertly and chased after it. Steadying, she raised her polo stick behind her and hit the ball some twenty metres towards the goal posts.

She cantered forward as the pack of players closed in on her. She raised her stick again and brought it down. But she missed the ball and cantered past it.

Another member of the blue team hit the ball, but a red defender was now positioned in front of the goal and as the ball approached him he took a mighty swipe and knocked it back down the pitch. The whistle blew for the end of the chukka.

Rose turned round to Sophia's father. "That wasn't bad. At least she had a hit."

Mr Gilbert's shoulders slumped. "But she missed a shot at an open goal."

After Sophia's match, which her team lost by one goal, two more teams rode onto the pitch. They were led by a stunning chestnut horse, which raised its reddish-brown head proudly, as it stood in front of the tents and admired the crowd.

"The captain for the green team is Jasper Armitage," announced Dickie. The athletic

Jasper raised his hand in acknowledgement as his chestnut horse pawed the ground.

"And the captain of the yellow team is Felix Kamau." Felix, a lean African man, rode a bay horse whose brown coat shone in the sunlight.

Both teams trotted and cantered their horses to warm up their muscles until the umpire blew his whistle and they lined up before him. Play began, and the ball sped in one direction and then back in the other.

Jasper rode his horse beautifully and was his team's key player. Each time the yellow team, led in their attack by Felix, hit the ball towards the green goal, Jasper charged forward and effortlessly struck it back up the pitch.

On several occasions, he followed the ball and played it the entire length of the pitch. He scored two goals for his team in the first three chukkas.

The yellow team was clearly frustrated, and Rose watched Felix remonstrate with them.

For the fourth and final chukka, Jasper changed back onto his smart chestnut horse. Felix hit a long ball towards his goal and raced after it. Jasper sped forward and the two met at the ball.

There was a scuffle, and a crack, and the ball ricocheted to the side. Jasper immediately leapt off his horse, which held a front leg up in the air.

Dickie leant across his wife and said urgently, "Rose, we better see if we can help. I hope Boadicea isn't seriously injured."

Rose followed Dickie onto the pitch and met Jasper as he led his hobbling horse to the sideline.

The umpire cantered towards them and sat back in his saddle as he pulled his horse to an abrupt stop. "Can you jump on one of your other ponies so we can finish the chukka, Jasper? There's only two minutes left and you still have the lead."

Rose took hold of Boadicea's bridle as Dickie said to Jasper, "Don't worry. We'll look after her while you finish the match."

A syce ran onto the pitch leading a brown horse. Jasper jumped on, glanced back at his chestnut mare, and cantered away.

Play continued as Dickie held Boadicea and Rose examined her leg. Her front knee had swollen and was hot and puffy under Rose's touch.

"She must have been hit by a stick or the ball," observed Dickie.

"Probably the ball as it shot sideways. It'll be impossible to tell if the bone has been chipped or cracked until the swelling subsides. But she won't be able to play for at least a month."

"Poor Jasper, he's down to two horses so he won't be able to play in the Mug's Mug next weekend."

"Unless he can find a replacement. He mentioned buying one from Brian Ellison."

Sophia Gilbert and her father joined them. "Can I help?" asked Sophia.

"Can you hold Boadicea? I need to ring the final bell," Dickie said, as he handed the reins to Sophia.

Her father squatted down next to Rose. "I know very little about horses, but that looks nasty. Do you need anything?"

Rose looked across at him gratefully. "Can you fetch my veterinary bag? I left it under the table where Dickie has his bell and microphone."

Mr Gilbert left and Rose heard the bell ring to signify the end of the final chukka. She looked up as Felix Kamau trotted towards her.

Jasper cantered up to him and stopped his horse sharply alongside Felix. "Why did you do that? Look at Boadicea, her knee's the size of a football and she's hopping about on three legs."

"It's not my fault," exclaimed Felix. "I caught your stick, and you snatched it away. You must have hit the ball at an angle."

"I'm reporting you to the steward for dangerous play," vented Jasper.

Rose noted that everyone around her had stopped to watch the altercation. "Mr Gilbert," she called. "My bag, please."

Mr Gilbert dragged his gaze away from the arguing players and delivered Rose's veterinary bag. He looked back as the mounted umpire rode up to Jasper and Felix.

"That's enough. Felix, your play was aggressive. Watch yourself. Jasper, I'm sorry about your horse, but it wasn't a foul, just an unfortunate accident."

"But look at her," Jasper beseeched, pointing toward Boadicea.

"I said, that's enough," repeated the umpire.

"Is there anything I can do to help?" asked Felix.

"I think you've done enough," spat Jasper. "Perhaps you should think carefully about continuing to play polo. This time it's a horse but the next time it might be a person ... or a child."

Felix dropped his polo stick. He slid off his horse, picked it up, and walked back across the polo pitch. His shoulders slumped as he dragged his horse behind him.

Jasper dismounted, handed his horse to his syce, and joined Rose. Gingerly, he touched Boadicea's swollen knee. She turned her head and bared her teeth at him.

"What do you think?" he asked Rose.

"That we need to hose it with cold water." Rose rummaged around in her bag. "And I'll inject her with some Phenylbutazone to reduce the swelling."

Rose stood. "I'm afraid she won't be fit to ride next weekend."

CHAPTER SIX

R ose accompanied Poppy and Dickie Chambers back to the clubhouse at the Timau Polo Grounds on Saturday evening.

At seven o'clock it was almost dark, but the temperature was still pleasantly warm so many of the polo players, and some of the polo club members, were standing or sitting at wooden picnic benches in a concrete courtyard beside the clubhouse. Behind the courtyard was a block containing the kitchen, showers and toilets.

"Shall we start with a drink?" suggested Dickie.

"Lovely," replied Rose. "A glass of white wine, please."

"Dickie, dear," said Poppy. "Why don't you buy a bottle for Rose and me to share."

"Good idea," he said, and disappeared inside the brick clubhouse.

At the far end of the courtyard, two BBQs glowed and some of the younger polo players congregated around them drinking from bottles of Tusker beer. Rose spotted Otto Wakeman's white-blonde curly locks.

Felix Kamau was sitting on the wall beside an attractive African woman whose gold jewellery twinkled when it caught the light of the BBQ. All the tables were occupied, but Rose spotted space beside Sophia Gilbert and her father.

"Do you mind if we join you?" asked Rose.

"Not at all," replied Sophia, smiling brightly at them.

Rose and Poppy sat down, and Rose continued to look around her. "The polo club's done a great job with the set-up here."

"I think they want to use the facility for other horse and community activities. I know the pony club is in discussion with Dickie at the moment," revealed Poppy.

"Come on, Dad, cheer up. It wasn't all bad today. I even scored a goal in the final match."

Mr Gilbert took a swig of his red wine but didn't respond.

Sophie watched him and said, "I don't think you can drive back to your hotel in Nanyuki tonight. The road's not safe when it's dark, and you've had a lot to drink."

"I'll be fine." Mr Gilbert looked up, and Rose noted his red-rimmed eyes.

"No, you won't, Dad. You'd better join me in the guest cottage. I can sleep on the sofa."

"Here you are," said Dickie, as he placed a bottle of white wine on the table with two glasses. "I'll be back in a tick."

Dickie returned with a pint glass and a bottle of Whitecap beer. As he tipped his glass at an angle and slowly poured his beer into it, he said, "We'll have to find someone else to run the bar next weekend. Moses is too old and slow and

Ali's happy to work at the main polo ground, but he's refused to come here."

"The polo club members could work on a shift system," suggested Poppy.

Dickie sipped his beer and wiped his mouth with his handkerchief. "We've done that before, but it didn't work as most of them forgot to come at their allotted times. No, I need to look for a couple of bartenders."

Poppy scratched her neck. "Debbie is away at the coast, so we'll also need some help with the food. I think the members can provide most of the dishes for lunch, but we need to provide afternoon teas as well."

Rose thought of her young friends. Chloe, together with Thabiti's sister Pearl, and their friend Marina, were planning to open a deli and small cafe in Nanyuki beside Dr Emma's new veterinary practice. Providing food for the polo club would be an excellent marketing opportunity.

"I know some young people who might be able to help. Let me speak to them."

"Thank you. That would be a relief," replied Poppy, gratefully.

The erect figure of Yaro Macharia stepped out of the clubhouse and looked around.

Beside Rose, Sophia looked at her father with concern and said, "Come on, Dad, I think it's time to go back to Wild Dog Estate."

Mr Gilbert extended his hand across the table and laid it on Sophia's as he said, "I'm sorry. I don't know what's the matter with me tonight. Do you think you could find me a coffee before we leave?"

Sophia stood, and Yaro stepped aside to let her into the clubhouse.

Rose followed Yaro's gaze, which was fixed on the crowd around the BBQs. There was much frivolity, and the attractive woman beside Felix leaned her head back and laughed.

Yaro marched across to the group and grabbed the woman by the wrist, dragging her off the wall.

She snatched her hand away and smoothed down her dress. "What was that for?" she demanded.

"Go inside," ordered Yaro.

"No, why should I? I'm enjoying myself out here. These boys are fun and at least they still play polo."

Yaro clenched his hands and his voice was menacing as he stated, "There's a reason for that, isn't there, Felix? Now go inside, Jasmine."

The woman gathered her bag and jacket and flounced past Rose's table into the clubhouse.

Felix jumped down from the wall and half-raised his hands in a gesture of surrender. "What happened four years ago in Nairobi was tragic, but it was an accident."

"Like today?" demanded Yaro. "I'm not sure I see it that way, and I doubt Jasper does either. And is chatting up my wife an accident?"

"She said she was bored with conversations about polo rules and sponsorship. Honestly, Yaro, I was only keeping her company while you were busy with polo committee work."

Yaro turned on his heels and strode back into the clubhouse. He soon reappeared, guiding his wife by the elbow. They walked past the now silent group around the BBQs and Rose soon heard the deep roar of a twin-turbo Land Cruiser engine.

Sophia placed a cup and saucer on the table and sat down opposite her father. His head was bowed. He looked up and his red-rimmed eyes were more pronounced and his skin had a grey pallor. "Can we just go back to the cottage?"

In a quiet voice Sophia replied, "Of course, if that's what you want."

It was completely dark beyond the polo club and there was a chill in the air.

"Shall we grab some meat from the BBQ and take it inside?" suggested Dickie.

Rose took two chicken skewers and followed Poppy into the clubhouse. Bread, salad and accompaniments were set out on a table beside the door. Rose added some coleslaw, lettuce and some mozzarella, tomato and basil salad to her plate and joined Dickie at a table beside the roaring log fire.

A group of young men came in and gathered at the end of the bar. "Another round," ordered Felix Kamau.

"Make mine a double whisky if Felix is buying," called a young man with a swarthy Mediterranean complexion.

Rose turned to Poppy and asked, "Who's that with the tan and straight, dark hair?"

"Rufus Esposito. He works for one of the flower farms outside Timau," Poppy replied.

"He's not a bad polo player," added Dickie. "But he's undisciplined and prone to losing his temper. It must be the Italian side of him."

"Hold the whisky," growled Jasper Armitage, his stocky, athletic figure rigid.

Rufus approached Jasper and draped his arm around his shoulder. "Come on Jasp. A man's got to have some fun."

Jasper lifted Rufus's arm off his shoulder. "I think you've had enough fun for one day."

'But it's still early," Impulsively, Rufus raised his arms. "Isn't it Otto?" he called to his fair-haired friend.

Jasper lowered one of Rufus's arms and said in a serious tone, "Your play today was erratic, and you were goggling so hard at Sophia that you let her slip past you and score."

Jasper's face softened and he let go of Rufus. "I'm just saying that you need to play better tomorrow if you want to be chosen for a team for next week's tournament. There are plenty of other players vying for places."

Rufus laughed and slapped Jasper's arm. "But you'll have me in your team, won't you?"

"I might not have a team," replied Jasper.

CHAPTER SEVEN

Rose arrived at Timau Polo Grounds at half-past nine on Sunday morning. She wanted to check on Jasper Armitage's polo ponies, Boadicea, and the palomino, Trigger, who had been transported to the Timau stables before the polo matches started.

Jasper's syce removed the top pole from a stable door and led Trigger out. Rose ran her hand down the horse's back leg and said, "I can't feel any heat or swelling." She asked the syce, "Are you still cooling it with cold water?"

He nodded. "I use bucket and towels, in the morning and before his tea."

Jasper joined them and added, "He's sound when we walk him out, until he turns sharply or walks across uneven ground."

Rose stood back and surveyed Trigger. "It's so frustrating, especially when you are short of horses. But riding him now could cause permanent damage."

"I know," responded Jasper glumly. "I would never do that."

The syce removed both entrance poles before leading out Boadicea. She tossed her elegant chestnut head, but it was clear her knee troubled her. She walked stiffly and rested her front leg when she stood for Rose to inspect her.

"The swelling is obvious," said Rose, "and there is still some heat. Have you been cold hosing it?"

"Yesterday," said the syce. "But I treat Trigger this morning, and get other ponies ready. I hose it now."

Rose watched the syce lead the reluctant Boadicea away, and observed, "You'll need another horse to play next weekend."

Jasper tapped his thigh. "I've just agreed to buy Brian Ellison's Excalibur. He's not as fast as he used to be, but he knows his job."

The lean figure of Felix Kamau walked past them with his head bowed. He wore his white polo breeches and carried his stick and helmet. He rounded the top of the stable block and Rose heard him shout, "Gathi. Gathi, why aren't my ponies ready?"

Jasper shook Rose's hand. "Thank you for your help. Did you receive the M-Pesa I sent on Thursday?"

"I did. Thank you for paying so promptly."

"I'll send some more later today, before my bill gets too large. But now I must get ready, as I'm umpiring today."

Rose picked up her veterinary bag and walked around the end of the stable block.

Felix emerged from the concrete storeroom beside his stables and asked, "Have you seen Gathi? He's supposed to have my horses ready."

A red-eyed Gathi slouched towards them. His clothes were crumpled and as he neared them Rose could smell alcohol. She pinched her lips.

"Why aren't my ponies ready?" demanded Felix. "I'm playing in the first match."

Gathi shrugged his shoulders. "Sorry, boss." He turned towards the storeroom and tripped over a broom lying on the floor.

"That's it. You're sacked."

Gathi got gingerly to his feet, brushing straw off his clothes. "Come on, boss. I'm only slightly late. Give me a chance."

Felix's nostrils flared as he exclaimed, "A chance. How many more do you want? I took a chance employing you in the first place. Everyone warned me against it. Said you were a hopeless drunk, but I felt sorry for you, and offered you this job. But you are a drunk. And you stink. Get out of here."

Felix took hold of Gathi and led him away from the stables to a mound of straw, partially covered by a tarpaulin. Gathi slumped down and as Felix strode away, he shook a fist and called, "You'll pay for this." He collapsed onto the straw and fell asleep.

Sophia emerged from Red's stable, holding a body brush. She placed it in a basket and walked towards Felix. "Can I help? I've only one match today, and it isn't until after lunch."

Rose placed her veterinary bag on the floor beside the storeroom. "And I can hold or lead a horse."

"Thank you," said Felix gratefully. "If I put the saddles and bridles outside each pony's stable, can you tack them up and bring them across? I'll get Noddy ready now and ride him across for the first chukka."

Sophia helped Felix tack up a bay horse. When they'd finished, Felix led him out of the stable and jumped on him. Rose passed Felix his polo stick, and he trotted away between the rows of stables.

"Can you hand me that bridle?" Sophia asked from inside a stable.

Rose did as requested and asked, "How's your father this morning?"

"He was rather sheepish. I made him coffee before I left and he kept apologising. It's such a shame. These outings are a real break for him away from Nairobi, from work, from Violet."

"Violet?" Rose queried.

"His wife, second wife. Can you pass the tendon boots?" Sophia squatted down and slipped a boot around the horse's front leg. "My mother died when I was little. Dad was devastated and threw himself into his work. Then Violet joined his company. She was cheerful and lively and gradually she drew him out of his gloominess.

"For a few years, they were really happy, until Violet had an accident. She's never fully recovered, and she needs full-time care. And if she finds alcohol, she drinks the lot and makes herself sick. Dad checks her into the Nairobi Centre for treatment whenever he comes to see me at the weekends."

"Did he drink too much?"

"Yes, and that's the thing. He rarely has more than one beer these days and only when he's out with other people. Because of Violet, he doesn't keep any alcohol in the house."

"Let's hope he feels better this afternoon, and comes to watch your match."

They pulled the three horses out of their stables and Sophia checked their tack. She put her foot in a stirrup and pulled herself up onto one pony, took the reins for the other two and rode away, leading the two ponies behind her.

CHAPTER EIGHT

O n Tuesday morning, Rose leaned against the uneven post-and-rail fence which surrounded her small field, which was part of the five-acre plot where she lived on the edge of Nanyuki. Bette, her cow, grazed peacefully under the branches and hazy green leaves of a Cape Chestnut tree.

"Slow down," she called to Chumba, a young African boy, as he rode past her on a grey pony.

Rose heard someone approach and looked back towards her one-bedroom thatched cottage. Each time she saw it, she felt a sense of peace.

Just over a month ago, she'd discovered her landlord was about to evict her and sell the property to buy a house in Nairobi for his daughter. But Thabiti, and his sister Pearl, had invested money from the trust fund their mother had left them to buy the cottage and its surrounding land.

Thabiti said it was a sound investment in a growing town, but promised not to build new houses on her field until she no longer needed it for her animals.

Kipto joined her beside the fence, and said, "Chumba do well. Better than his school work."

Chumba was Kipto's grandson and he was twelve years old.

"He's very confident, perhaps a little too much so. Like most boys, he enjoys going fast," remarked Rose. "Chumba, slow down and gather up your reins. They're hanging like washing lines."

Chumba trotted towards them and pulled hard on his reins to slow his pony, Bahati, before he reached the fence.

Bahati meant luck in Swahili, although the pony had precious little of it until the KSPCA, Kenya Society for the Protection and Care of Animals, had rescued him from beside a busy Nairobi road. He had been covered in sores and swellings and was still nervous about being handled.

"Ride him steadily and collectedly for one more circuit," Rose instructed the boy.

As Chumba turned his pony and trotted away, she said to Kipto, "Chumba's really gelled with that pony. Samwell can't get near him, but Chumba was nearly under Bahati's tummy yesterday as he brushed his legs."

Rose felt a vibration in her pocket. She removed her mobile phone and answered, "Habari."

"Hi, Rose. It's Chloe. I got your message about catering at the polo club next weekend. Do you have any more details?"

"I don't, but I'll send you Poppy Chambers' number. You've met her at East Africa Women's League meetings and she's in charge of the catering for the polo club."

"Thanks. Then I can discuss it with the others. Talking of which, are you free for lunch? Thabiti's received a message from Sam that Judy, Constable Wachira, has passed her sergeant's exams."

"That's wonderful. I'm so pleased for her," replied Rose.

"She doesn't want any fuss, but Commissioner Akida has given her the day off, and Sam is taking her for lunch at Cape Chestnut. And we think this calls for a proper celebration, so we're going to join them."

"Are you sure that's what she wants?" asked Rose.

Chloe chuckled. "It's too late now. Pearl has ordered a cake and asked for two bottles of prosecco to be put on ice. Will you join us?"

"I will, although I don't want to upset or embarrass Constable, or should I say, Sergeant Wachira."

Rose walked through the rickety wooden gate into the grounds of Cape Chestnut restaurant and followed the concrete-flagged path past the single-storey, colonial style restaurant building.

Her friends were not seated on the veranda but at a long wooden table under the shade of a large Cape Chestnut tree, after which the restaurant was named.

Pearl and Chloe were sitting at the far side of the table and were partially hidden by a large bouquet of pink roses. A silver helium balloon bobbed in the air with 'Congratulations' printed on it. Rose noted it was anchored to a small box beside the flowers.

She sat down next to Marina, an Indian girl in her early twenties, who was friendly with Pearl and Chloe. Rose was unsure whether she was just friends with Thabiti, who sat next to her, or if there was more to their relationship.

Rose asked, "How was Kakuma?" Marina had been working as a volunteer at the huge refugee camp in the desert area of northern Kenya for six weeks, as a volunteer.

"I enjoyed it, but I'm pleased to be back. After a while you begin to think that whatever you do, you can't really help the people there."

Thabiti turned and placed a hand over Marina's. "Don't be hard on yourself. I saw the affectionate way everyone greeted you, and I'm sure the children will be missing you."

"And I heard you helped one of the refugees start a small cafe," prompted Rose.

"Yes, a young man called Nathaniel, who was originally from Rwanda. He'd lost his entire family and ended up at Kakuma, after being moved from a camp in Tanzania. He'd worked various jobs to earn enough money to open the cafe and his determination and enterprise were inspiring."

"So much so that you're now leading the cafe project for our retail enterprise," declared Pearl.

"And you have loads of contacts in Nairobi for interesting products to sell in our deli," added Chloe.

Pearl jumped up and announced, "Here she comes."

Rose turned as the diminutive and attractive Sergeant Wachira was chaperoned to their table by Sam, a huge bald-headed bear of a man. Sam had worked for Kenya's Anti-Poaching Unit, but he'd recently left the Kenya Wildlife Service to become Operations Director for Ol Pejeta Conservancy.

Rose had become friends with him and Sergeant Wachira as they'd investigated various murders together in Laikipia, and Sam and Rose had even solved a case in Kenya's iconic Maasai Mara.

"Congratulations," called Chloe and Pearl in unison.

Sergeant Wachira's ears coloured and she smiled nervously. "You really shouldn't have, but thank you."

She and Sam sat down opposite Pearl and Chloe.

Marina turned to Rose and said, "Chloe gave me Poppy Chambers' number and I rang her about catering at the polo tournament. Thank you for suggesting us."

"Are you going to do it?"

"Yes. She'd like us to provide cold meats and quiches for the lunches and afternoon teas. I can easily make sandwiches, but I'm not great at baking."

Chloe leaned towards them. "I spoke to Dotty, who's staying with us. She and Agnes, my house girl, have been entrenched in the kitchen for the last few days. Yesterday they produced a fabulous lemon drizzle cake and some scones. She said she'd be happy to help with the baking, and teach Agnes."

Chloe lowered her voice. "I think she's delighted to have something meaningful to do. And she blushes whenever she's complimented. Her husband treats her like a house girl, and simply ignores her when Dan is around."

Marina wrinkled her lips before remarking in an overly bright tone, "Poppy Chambers also said her husband is looking for bar tenders for the weekend. What do you think, Thabiti?"

"Me," he blurted. "I don't think so."

"What if I join you?" suggested Sam, who was seated next to Thabiti. Sam looked around the table. "Marina, if you're busy with the food, then the rest of us could pitch in and run the bar. I have to be there anyway as I'm running a stall promoting Ol Pejeta Conservancy."

"That sounds like a great idea," exclaimed Pearl. "I've always wondered what happens at polo matches. They seem so... colonial."

CHAPTER NINE

On Wednesday morning, Rose parked next to the stables at the Timau Polo Grounds. Chumba jumped out of the passenger seat, ran towards the horses and stroked the head of one, as Rose closed the car door.

The crumpled figure of Gathi approached her. He held his hands out in a begging gesture as he pleaded, "Please Mama, you give me job?"

Rose shook her head. "No, Gathi. I don't need any more help. You had a perfectly good job, and you lost it. I doubt anyone in the polo community will employ you now. I'm sorry, but you need to sort yourself out... and stop drinking away the money you do earn."

Rose spotted Gathi's former employer, Felix Kamau, holding his horse by the reins and trying to return his saddle to the storeroom at the end of his row of stables. Chumba dashed across and took hold of the horse.

Felix emerged from the storeroom as Rose joined him and Chumba. "Thank you, young man. I need someone with your enthusiasm."

Rose tilted her head and asked, "Do you need help this weekend?"

"One of my syces is coming up with a horse I've just bought from Brian Ellison, but I'm still short-handed. Why? Are you suggesting I take Gathi back?"

Rose glanced behind her and murmured, "Not at all." In a louder voice, she continued, "But Chumba is on his school holidays. He can ride and he helps me at home."

Felix took hold of the reins and led his horse to an empty stable. He pulled the bridle over his horse's ears and the bit fell out of its mouth. "So what do you think, Chumba? Would you like to be a syce for the Mugs Mug tournament? It'll be busy as I'm guaranteed to be playing both days."

Chumba nodded enthusiastically.

Felix chuckled. "Great, when can you start?"

"He can start now if you like. And I can send his things on a boda boda. What does he need?"

Felix walked back into the concrete storeroom and hung up his bridle. "He can sleep here on this mattress." Felix pointed to the wooden platform above the saddles. "So all he needs is some bedding, clothes and eating utensils. There's a local man providing food for all the syces."

Rose left the storeroom and spoke seriously to Chumba. "Are you happy to do this? You don't have to."

"They lovely horses," he replied as he stroked the brown head of the horse in the stable next to him.

Rose turned to Felix. "Let me know if you have any problems. But I'm sure you'll be fine. He's a good boy."

Rose walked around the back of the storeroom and down the adjacent row of stables. Trigger, Jasper Armitage's palomino horse, shook his head at her. In the neighbouring stable, the striking Boadicea stood with her head bowed.

Jasper's syce appeared looking sheepish. "I call master. He exercising Biscuit."

The syce entered Trigger's stable, pulled on the head collar and led the horse out of the stable. Rose ran her hand down Trigger's back legs. There was some swelling just below the hock joint of the right one.

Jasper appeared, riding a bay horse. He jumped off athletically and led it into an empty stable. Reappearing, he said, "He's still only lame on uneven or rough ground."

"There's some swelling now. I'll give him another shot of Flunixin, and your syce will need to continue with the cold water treatment."

As Rose prepared the anti-inflammatory injection, she asked Jasper, "When's your new horse arriving?"

Jasper crossed his arms. "It's not. For me at least." He glanced over the top of the stables, towards Felix's polo ponies. Chumba was singing as he brushed the horse Felix had recently ridden.

"Felix gazumped me and offered Brian a higher price. And he has the gall to play it this weekend. It's arriving with some other ponies from Nairobi, later today."

"So what are you going to do?" Rose rubbed the spot where she had injected Trigger and the syce led him back into his stable.

"I'm out of options for ponies, so Dickie has asked me to umpire."

The syce led Boadicea out of her stable. She looked apathetic, and her head drooped. Rose shook her head as she felt the mare's knee. "There's hardly any improvement. I'll also give her another shot of Flunixin and you should continue with the cold hosing. Are you leading her out at all?"

Jasper looked at his syce, who shook his head.

"I think, like Trigger, she needs walking twice a day. Don't take her too far, but let her graze. We'll see if that helps her knee, and her disposition."

"Take her out now," instructed Jasper. "I'll untack Biscuit."

"So who'll fill your place in your Mug's Mug team?" asked Rose as she watched Boadicea walk stiffly away.

"I've no idea. I've passed the captaincy over to Ed, so it's for him to decide. Just as long as he doesn't choose Felix," Jasper growled.

CHAPTER TEN

O n Friday morning, Thabiti drove Chloe, and her guest Dotty, to the North Kenya Polo Club to see the African wild dogs.

"I feel rather guilty leaving Marina and Pearl to see suppliers for the deli," revealed Chloe.

"I'm sorry, it's my fault. I really wanted to see the wild dogs after I watched a documentary about them," confessed Dotty.

"Ladies, there's no need to worry. Marina knows what you're looking for and I'm sure she'll get you a product list," said Thabiti. "I'm rather excited about seeing the wild dogs."

"And you're going to photograph, and film them?" asked Dotty, with a note of awe in her voice. "Like one of those wildlife photographers they feature after the main documentary."

Thabiti felt the heat rise in his face. "Not exactly. But the photos and video footage might come in useful." He braked as they reached the entrance gate to the polo club.

Dotty jumped out before Chloe had a chance to unclip her seat belt, and struggled to drag the gate open.

Once through, they drove alongside the conifer wood and turned right at the end onto the polo pitch. Thabiti's heart sunk. There was no sign of the wild dogs. He drove slowly along the edge of the pitch.

"Steady," said Chloe. "There's a large hole under the root of that lone fig tree, and I thought I saw something move."

Thabiti turned the steering wheel to the left, and they drove onto the pitch until he judged they were far enough away not to frighten the animals, but close enough to observe them. He opened his window and began to assemble his GoPro video camera.

Whilst they waited, Dotty removed the lid from a vacuum flask and asked, "Coffee?"

She handed out cups of coffee and passed around home-made oat biscuits.

"Thanks," mumbled Thabiti through a mouthful of biscuit.

Thabiti finished his biscuit and wiped his hands on his shorts. He was attaching the GoPro to the doorframe when he noticed movement at the entrance to the den, which was a dark hole surrounded by the exposed roots of the fig tree. The area in front was dusty brown earth.

Six adult dogs emerged and turned to face the entrance. Their white tails, which contrasted with the blotches of black and brown on their bodies, flicked from side to side as they waited. Thabiti screwed the lens on his camera and steadied his breathing.

"Oh, sweet," exclaimed Dotty in the back seat.

"What?" complained Chloe. "I can't see a thing." She got out of the car and walked around to stand by Dotty's open rear window.

Small puppies scrambled out of the hole, helped by two adult wild dogs. "That one with the exposed teats must be the mother," remarked Dotty. "She'll be the alpha female of the pack. The only one with the privilege of giving birth to pups."

"They're tiny," exclaimed Chloe. "Do you think this is the first time they've left their den?"

"Shush," urged Thabiti. "I'm filming and I don't want to hear you two chatting."

Thabiti checked his GoPro. If this was the pups' first foray into the world, his footage would be rare, and important to those who studied the most endangered carnivore in Africa, after the Ethiopian wolf.

He picked up his camera and took shot after shot as the pups explored and all the adults joined in, marshalling and assisting them. There truly was a strong bond between all the members of the pack.

After twenty minutes, the pups were herded back into the den. The alpha female stood outside and watched the rest of the pack trot away, presumably to hunt.

"Wow." Chloe's voice was breathless as she took another cup of coffee from Dotty.

Thabiti packed away his camera as the alpha female disappeared into the den. He got out of the car, took another biscuit, and walked around to stretch his legs.

"Were the pack going to look for food?" asked Chloe.

"I expect so," replied Thabiti. "I hope they don't target lambs or calves on nearby farms. Many farmers consider them pests or vermin and try to poison or shoot them."

"The pack can move fast and cover ten to twenty kilometres in a few hours," Dotty revealed.

"That would take them down to Gaia and Lewa conservancies. But how do they bring food back for the pups' mother?"

"They regurgitate it," responded Dotty.

"They do what?" exclaimed Chloe. "And how do you know so much about wild dogs?"

Dotty blushed and bowed her head. "I was so excited about our trip that I read and watched everything I could about Kenya, and Africa."

Chloe patted Dottie's arm. "Good for you. So how does the mother get fed?"

"The others eat the prey, but when they return, they regurgitate it for the female to eat. They'll do the same for the pups when they're ready to eat meat."

"Thank you, Dotty. That was certainly worth a visit," said Thabiti as he climbed back into the car.

CHAPTER ELEVEN

Thabiti drove into the drive of Chloe's single-storey brick house and parked beside the front door as Dan, Chloe's husband, and Dotty's husband, Al, walked out of it.

"I'm going to show Al around Nanyuki, and then we're meeting some army mates at Kongonis," announced Dan, as Thabiti, Dotty and Chloe extracted themselves from the car. "I'm not sure when we'll be back, so don't wait for us to have supper."

Dan pecked Chloe on the cheek and he and Al drove away in a long-wheelbase Land Rover Defender. Pearl walked out of the side door of the house and joined Chloe and Dotty while Thabiti unpacked the car.

Chloe watched the askari close the gate, and asked, in a preoccupied tone, "Dotty, do you have children?"

Dotty tugged at her long, tiered skirt, and replied, "Al already has a son and daughter, so he didn't want any more children."

Pearl looked enquiringly at Chloe but remained silent.

Chloe volunteered, "I'd like a family. Dan and I have been trying for a while but we've had... difficulties."

"But you seemed more positive after visiting the consultant in Nairobi," volunteered Pearl.

"I was, especially as she was doubtful about my previous diagnosis, that my body is rejecting the foetus. She thinks I'm short of progesterone, which is why she started me on a course of progesterone supplement medication. But it needs two people to make a baby and Dan's been rather preoccupied this week."

"I'm sorry," muttered Dotty. "That will be Al keeping him up late, talking and drinking whisky."

Thabiti felt the heat rising in his face as Marina joined him by the car and picked up the basket with the vacuum flask and remaining cookies."

Pearl announced, "I'm not sure I want kids, but I've had plenty of practice looking after Thabiti."

Thabiti looked up, "Oy!"

Pearl laughed, "Don't worry, I'm passing that responsibility on to Marina."

Marina's cheeks flushed as she carried the basket into the house, and Thabiti followed her.

Dotty joined them in the kitchen and washed her hands. "Are you ready to start cooking?" she asked Agnes, Chloe's house girl.

"I have all the ingredients you asked for here." She indicated with her hand towards a counter on which various baking products were laid out, including eggs, flour, sugar and chocolate.

Chloe walked in and placed her hands on the counter as she proclaimed, "Returning to our conversation, Marina and Thabiti. Are you two now an item?"

Thabiti felt the heat rise in his face again as he stammered, "I've got to meet Sam," and he bolted out of the kitchen.

Thabiti sat in the passenger seat of a long-wheelbase, safari style Land Cruiser which Sam had borrowed from Ol Pejeta Conservancy's.

They were driving north towards the Timau Polo Grounds and the vehicle was jam-packed. Sam was transporting a tent, banners and display boards to set up in readiness for marketing Ol Pejeta Conservancy to those attending the weekend's polo tournament.

Dickie Chambers had also asked them to collect wine and spirits from Settlers Store, for the bar which Sam, Thabiti and Pearl were running over the weekend. Judy had offered to lend a hand, as Marina was busy with the catering, and Chloe was helping her.

East African Breweries would deliver crates of beer directly to the polo ground, and Dickie had told them Coca Cola had already dropped off the soft drinks.

Sam parked at the rear of the clubhouse by a white ISO shipping container. To reduce the visual impact of the forty-foot-long metal storage container, some of the polo members and their friends had painted scenes on it. There was one with Mount Kenya and another of wildlife, including a pack of African wild dogs.

"Can you fetch the key for the padlock on the ISO container door from the clubhouse?" asked Sam. "Dickie told me he's hidden it at the back of the bar in a silver trophy."

Thabiti entered the concrete courtyard where a number of polo players were either sitting at, or standing beside, a wooden picnic table.

A tall man leaned against the end of the table and addressed a young man with dark Mediterranean features. "Rufus, I'm sorry, but your play is just too erratic. And you lost your temper again with the umpire last week. Jasper's umpiring this weekend, and he won't stand for such behaviour."

Rufus, who had been leaning against the clubhouse wall, stood up and looked across at a man whose long, fair curls fell over his face. Thabiti recognised Otto Wakeman, who was sitting at the picnic table.

Rufus pleaded, "Back me up, Otto. You can't want Felix Kamau in the Painted Dogs team instead of me. Not after what he did to Jasper with that horse."

Otto tapped the table but didn't look up as he replied, "Felix swears he had no idea Brian had already agreed to sell Excalibur to Jasper. But it's not my decision. Ed is captain now."

"I don't believe this," exclaimed Rufus as Thabiti walked into the clubhouse.

It took Thabiti a full five minutes to find the padlock key, as it was not in a silver trophy, but hanging behind a plaque on the wall above the bar.

When he finally emerged from the clubhouse he noted that a young, lean African man and an attractive long-legged girl had joined the group around the picnic table.

The tall man raised his hands and declared, "Sorry, I've made my decision." He looked at the African man. "Felix, you'll join the Painted Dogs team," he turned to Rufus, "and you'll stay in Only Fools on Horses."

As Thabiti walked past, Rufus stormed away with a murderous expression on his face. Although Felix had his arms loosely crossed, he looked content.

Thabiti heard the tall man ask, "So Sophia, would you like to join the Only Fools on Horses team?"

"Oh, yes, please," exclaimed a shrill female voice.

Sam had piled the cases of wine and boxes of spirits outside the container.

"Sorry, apologised Thabiti. The key wasn't in the trophy, so I had to hunt around for it."

"No problem," replied Sam as he unlocked the padlock and drew back the bolts on the metal door of the ISO container.

CHAPTER TWELVE

Rose arrived at the Timau Polo Grounds at a quarter past nine on Saturday morning, with the tournament due to commence at ten o'clock. She parked in the second row of cars next to the clubhouse.

The first person she met was the club chairman, Dickie Chambers. "Morning, Dickie," she said brightly.

"Ah, Rose. Yes. Morning." He looked past her and then from left to right.

Rose's eyebrows drew together. "What's the matter? Have you lost someone?"

"Something. We've lost something. One of the covers for the goal posts. Let me know if you see it."

He turned and walked purposely towards the kitchen, nearly bumping into Thabiti, who was carrying two cafetières of coffee.

Thabiti's gaze followed Dickie's retreating back. "Habari, Mama Rose. What's wrong with bwana Chambers?"

"I'm not sure. He said something about a missing goal post cover." She walked with Thabiti into the clubhouse.

Thabiti placed the cafetières on a trestle table and asked, "What's that?"

"Goal post covers are usually lengths of red and white-striped padded plastic which are wrapped around the posts to provide cushioning, and prevent injury to a horse and rider should they collide with the goal posts." Rose looked around for tea bags.

Marina arrived with a tray. "Morning, are you looking for tea?" She placed the tray on the table and unloaded an assortment of tea bags, sugar and biscuits.

Thabiti reached for a biscuit, but Marina grabbed his wrist. "These are for the guests. You can have a broken one from the kitchen. And Sam's arrived."

"I thought you were only doing afternoon tea, and a few lunch dishes," remarked Rose.

Marina lifted the tray and replied. "Poppy seemed overwhelmed, as someone had let her down, so we volunteered to organise all the food. We might as well, as we're here anyway."

Thabiti let Marina leave the clubhouse before adding in a disgruntled tone, "I'm not sure where the 'we' part came from. Anyway, I promised to help Sam set up the rest of his Ol Pejeta Conservancy stall."

Thabiti left and Rose made her tea and carried it out to the courtyard, where she sat down at one of the picnic tables.

More cars arrived.

Mr Gilbert, Sophia's father, ushered a frail-looking African woman to the adjacent picnic table and disappeared inside the clubhouse, returning with two cups.

"Here's your tea, my dear. But be careful, it's hot. Would you like a biscuit?" He held one up and she removed it suspiciously from his hand.

Dickie Chambers rushed down the bank leading to the main polo pitch.

He passed Sophia Gilbert, who was immaculately dressed in white polo breeches and a bright yellow polo shirt, with a red logo on the breast.

"Hello," she said nervously as she walked past Rose. "Dad," she bent down to kiss her father on the cheek, but hesitated as she looked up. "And Violet."

She frowned and lowered her voice. "Why have you brought Violet? You never bring her to polo matches, not after ... what happened."

Mr Gilbert examined his hands. Then he looked up and held Sophia's gaze. "She has to face reality sometime, to recognise what torments her."

Sophia stood up and placed her hands on her hips. "But this is a really important tournament. And they'll be loads of people here."

Mr Gilbert smiled weakly. "I know, but that might be better. She can retreat into the crowd. But it does mean I have to look after her rather than help you. How are you feeling?"

Sophia's arms dropped to her sides. "Excited, but my stomach feels as heavy as a rock. And what if I mess up and let the whole team down? And there are selectors here to choose a women's team to tour India this autumn."

Mr Gilbert's smile widened and his voice was energised. "A trip to India, that would be fantastic."

"Dad, don't raise your hopes. There are far better players than me."

"But still, since you're in a team, you have a chance. Let's have a look at your team shirt."

Sophia turned her back to him. Her shirt bore a number '3' and above it the words, 'Only Fools on Horses'.

Sophia turned back to face her father and bit her lip. She asked, "What do you think?"

He placed a hand on her arm. "It's great. Now just concentrate on your game. How is your new horse?"

Sophia's shoulders relaxed. "He's amazing and I'm really getting the hang of him. Felix has been helping me, but I hope he's not too keen in my matches."

Mr Gilbert's eyes narrowed as he responded, "You be careful."

"I'd better go." Sophia kissed her father's cheek, turned on her heel and jogged down the bank towards the main polo pitch.

Thabiti appeared carrying a red crate of rattling bottles, which he rested on Rose's table. "I might have found that red and white cover thing Bwana Chambers is looking for."

"Show me," directed Rose, placing her hands on the table and pushing herself upright.

She followed Thabiti around the back of the ISO container to an area piled with rubbish and empty crates. There was something red underneath a haphazard heap of cardboard boxes. Thabiti removed several and Rose leaned down and felt the exposed thick padded plastic.

"I think this is it. Well done." She helped Thabiti remove more boxes until he was able to pull the cover free. They returned to the courtyard with Thabiti carrying the goal post cover over his shoulder.

"You found it," exclaimed Dickie. He wiped his brow with a green paisley handkerchief. "Where was it?"

"In a pile of rubbish behind the clubhouse," replied Rose.

Thabiti deposited the cover on the table with a thump and picked up his crate of bottles. "It looked as if someone had deliberately hidden it." He disappeared inside the clubhouse.

"Who would do that?" Dickie's tone was indignant.

"A disgruntled player ... or syce," replied Rose thoughtfully.

Dickie wrapped his arms around the cover and lifted it off the table. "I need to attach this to the post, as play starts in fifteen minutes. I was thinking that we should unveil Craig's portrait at tea time. Is that OK with you?"

Dickie had commissioned a portrait of her husband in recognition of his many years of support, and work as Treasurer, for the North Kenya Polo Club.

"Of course," replied Rose, as she sat down to finish her tea.

Three black Land Cruisers, with tinted windows, drew up to the entrance of the clubhouse courtyard. Four large African men extracted themselves from the front and back vehicles and looked around, and one opened the rear door of the middle car.

A distinguished looking African couple climbed out, both wearing a considerable amount of heavy gold jewellery.

Mr Gilbert stood up and approached Rose. In a quiet voice, he asked, "Who's that? I recognise the man."

Rose leant towards him. "Kristopher Kamau, and his wife. He's a long-standing politician, and Felix Kamau's father."

Mr Gilbert drew in his breath and looked uneasy.

Mr and Mrs Kamau were escorted down the bank towards No. 2 pitch by their minders.

"Excuse me," Rose said to Mr Gilbert. "I think the first match is about to start."

CHAPTER THIRTEEN

As Rose stopped at the entrance to the members' tent, beside No. 2 pitch, she wondered if the muffled conversations and surreptitious glances were caused by the arrival of Mr and Mrs Kamau.

She turned and stepped to one side as she watched the first two teams line up, facing the members' tent.

Dickie Chambers announced, "The opening match of this year's Mugs Mug tournament will be between the Painted Dogs, wearing dark brown, and Only Fools on Horses, wearing yellow."

Dickie introduced the players. Felix Kamau and Otto Wakeman were both on the Painted Dogs team and Rose noted the head of a wild dog printed on the front of their polo shirts.

Sophia Gilbert was riding her new horse, Red, for the Only Fools on Horses team, and he appeared excited by the prospect of the match and kept rushing backwards and throwing his head about.

Dickie finished introducing the players, and they wheeled around and cantered away.

"And the umpire for this match is Jasper Armitage. He has kindly volunteered this weekend after injuries to two of his top ponies. I'm sure you'll join me in wishing them a speedy recovery."

The players formed two lines facing each other and Jasper bowled the ball between them as play commenced.

Rose stopped at a stall selling hand-woven carpets. "Habari," she greeted the two elderly African women who attended the major tournaments each year, travelling from Meru, an hour further north, to sell their wares.

Rose heard the pounding of hooves and looked up. Sophia was riding towards the ball with her polo stick raised. Felix Kamau drew alongside and his horse made contact with Red.

Red's ears flicked back, and he sped forward. Too fast, as he galloped over the top of the ball. Otto Wakeman, who'd been chasing Sophia and Felix, whacked the ball back down the pitch.

Rose heard one of the players swear at Sophia.

"Enough of that language, Rufus, or I will send you off," shouted Jasper, who was standing up in his stirrups. "And don't you think you should encourage your fellow team members, rather than berate them?"

As play continued at the far end of the pitch, Rose noted Sophia holding back the prancing Red.

Beyond the line of stalls, a young voice shouted, "Simama."

She thought it sounded like Chumba, and both Sam and Thabiti emerged from the end stall. Rose walked quickly towards the cry, and as she rounded the corner of the Ol Pejeta Conservancy tent, she saw Sam approach Gathi, who was trying to wrestle the reins of a polo pony away from Chumba.

"What's going on?" demanded Sam in a deep drawl.

Chumba looked around helplessly. "He won't let go of my horse. And Master Felix needs him for the next chukka." He looked up and locked eyes with Rose. "Mama, please tell him to stop."

Sam glanced round as Rose approached the group, and then turned back to Gathi and declared, "I don't know who you are, but let go of this horse."

The bell sounded and Felix trotted towards them and called, "Quick Chumba, bring me Noddy."

"I can't, Gathi won't let go of his reins."

Sam growled and Gathi jumped back, releasing his grip.

Chumba tugged Noddy's reins and dragged him towards Felix, who had jumped off his horse and was running beside it towards Chumba. They swapped horses and as the bell sounded, Felix jumped on Noddy and cantered onto the pitch.

Gathi slouched away.

"Are you OK?" Rose asked Chumba.

"Yes, asanti." He looked up at Sam with wide eyes. "Gathi, try to get me in trouble all the time. He hides things, like my blankets," Chumba mumbled.

Rose's muscles tightened. "Were you all right? It's cold here at night."

"I borrowed one of the horse rugs." Chumba looked down at his feet.

Sam squatted down and lifted Chumba's chin. He kept eye contact with the boy as he instructed, "You tell me if he causes any more trouble. I'll soon sort him out."

Chumba's mouth broke into a wide grin. "Asanti, bwana." He led Felix's horse to a post-and-rail fence, picked up a lead rein which was tied to it, and clipped it onto the bridle. He lifted a bucket to the horse's mouth and Rose heard it slurping water.

Rose, Thabiti and Sam retreated to the Ol Pejeta Conservancy stall.

Out on the polo pitch, play continued at a frenetic pace. The ball raced towards Sophia, who knocked it back and trotted forward in pursuit. Felix galloped towards her and turned his horse sharply, crashing into the side of her horse.

"Ow," blurted Thabiti. "That wasn't very nice."

Jasper blew his whistle. He rode up to Felix and shouted, "That was completely unnecessary, overly aggressive behaviour."

"Watching that incident, you wouldn't believe Felix has been helping Sophia all week," Rose commented to Thabiti and Sam. "Some completely reasonable players ride onto a polo pitch and, when the match starts, their personalities change completely."

"You idiot," shouted Rufus as Sophia missed the penalty drop.

"And some players," continued Rose, "are naturally uncouth."

CHAPTER FOURTEEN

Rose walked down to No. 2 pitch with Poppy Chambers to watch the second of the afternoon's polo matches. Rufus, with his swarthy features, stood outside the members' tent with another polo player.

Sophia joined them, and Rufus draped an arm around her shoulders and whispered in her ear. She wriggled free, said something Rose could not catch and strode up the bank towards Rose and Poppy.

"Have you seen my father?" Sophia enquired.

"I'm afraid not, and he wasn't in the clubhouse when we left. Didn't he watch your last match?"

"I hope so, which is why I thought he'd be in the members' tent. I need a cold drink so I'll check in the clubhouse again." She strode away up the bank.

Rufus and his friend stopped giggling as Rose and Poppy reached the members' tent and took their places inside. The two men followed and sat several rows behind as the next two polo teams lined up on the pitch.

Felix Kamau was riding a lovely steel-grey coloured horse which stood calmly with its ears pricked.

Poppy whispered, "That's Excalibur, Brian Ellison's old polo pony. It's very experienced, although a little slower than it used to be."

Jasper Armitage, wearing the black and white vertically striped umpire's shirt, rode onto the pitch astride a strawberry roan horse.

"Is that Sophia's horse, Red, which she also bought from Brian?" asked Poppy.

Jasper pulled on the reins to bring his horse to a stop and although it slowed down, it threw its head around.

"Yes, I believe so," replied Rose.

As the players began to warm up their horses, ready for the match, Mr Gilbert, Violet and Sophia sat down next to Rose and Poppy.

Sophia said, "I hope Red behaves. Jasper said he'd ride him, to take the edge off. But Red's just fighting him."

Mr Gilbert turned to Sophia and said in an apologetic tone, "You were right, we should have taken Excalibur. He might be slower, and he doesn't have Red's presence, but he's been very reliable for Felix Kamau today."

Sophia placed a hand on her father's leg and replied, "I love Red, he's such a character. I just need more practice, and more match experience. Just wait, we'll be a fantastic combination next season." She leaned across to Violet and asked, "What do you think? Do you like my new pony?"

Jasper cantered up to the tent and cried, "Can you throw me a ball?" Red's nostrils were flaring, and he shook his head from side to side in a savage manner.

Violet shrank back and started to whimper.

Mr Gilbert put his arm around her shoulder. "There, there, it's all right. That's Sophia's new horse." Mr Gilbert sounded as if he was speaking to a child and not a grown woman.

Dickie Chambers threw Jasper the ball and he cantered away. Play started.

A head appeared and disappeared around the corner of the tent. Was that Gathi still hanging around and being a nuisance?

Rose turned to Sophia. "Why don't you ask Felix if you can swap horses until the end of the season? He's a good horseman, and you'd learn a lot riding Excalibur."

Rufus called from the back, "Don't you let Felix anywhere near your horse, otherwise you might find he's injured it, claimed it as his own or let it loose to cause havoc."

Dickie stood and rang the bell. There was no sound. He turned the bell over and exclaimed, "Who's stolen the clapper from my bell? And how do I stop play now?"

Rufus called out again. "Why don't you take your top off and run onto the pitch, Soph? That's would certainly grab the players' attention."

Mr Gilbert turned around, red-faced, and barked, "Don't be so disgusting."

Rufus and his friend sniggered.

Sophia jumped up, gave Rufus a thunderous look, and stormed onto the pitch.

"Oh, ay," called Rufus after her and attempted a half-hearted whistle.

Sophie put her fingers in her mouth and made a loud and strident wolf whistle. The players reined their horses to a stop and stared at her.

"End of the first chukka," she said sweetly, and returned to the tent.

Felix rode past and called, "Where did you learn to do that, Sophia?"

"A private education in South Africa," she yelled back.

Rufus walked out of the tent. His face was flushed and his jaw was set.

Sophia met her father at the entrance with a trembling Violet. "I'll take her back to the clubhouse for a cup of tea. I've organised a bed for her in a wing of the Cottage Hospital tonight so I can come back for the party. And I've brought a sleeping bag, so can I borrow your sofa?"

CHAPTER FIFTEEN

P oppy and Rose walked steadily up the bank, away from No. 2 polo pitch towards the clubhouse.

Sophia and Felix Kamau strode ahead of them. "The party tonight should be fun," said Sophia. "Even my Dad's coming. And he's found somewhere to look after Violet."

"Who is Violet? And what's the matter with her?"

Sophia stopped and dropped her voice. As Rose walked past, she heard her whisper, "She's Dad's second wife. His first, my mum, died years ago. Poor Violet suffers terribly from depression and anxiety. And she was such a bubbly woman before she lost her baby."

Rose and Poppy reached the courtyard and Poppy said, "I'm going to check if Marina and her gang are ready to serve afternoon tea." She left in the direction of the kitchen, weaving through the crowd of people.

Felix and Sophia joined Mr Gilbert and Violet, who were sitting at a picnic table at the edge of the throng.

Sophia began, "Felix, can I introduce my father, Laurie, and his wife, Violet."

Laurie Gilbert offered his hand but Felix didn't take it as his own father called, "Felix, over here."

Felix smiled apologetically at Sophia and joined his parents, who were standing with the attractive Jasmine Macharia, Yaro's wife.

Yaro walked out of the clubhouse, but stopped and stared at his wife.

Thabiti pushed through the crowd lugging a crate of Tusker beers. "Excuse me," he said to Felix and Jasmine.

Felix placed his hand on the small of Jasmine's back and pulled her to one side.

"Thank you," mumbled Thabiti.

Yaro, his face set, stepped back into the clubhouse, and Thabiti followed him.

Jasper Armitage, who still wore the striped umpire's shirt, approached Sophia and shook hands with her father. He squatted down, took Violet's hand and whispered something to her. An inkling of a smile appeared on her face.

Jasper stood and said, "I loved riding Red today, but he does like to get his own way. It's so frustrating I can't play, especially as the selectors arrived this afternoon."

Sophia's eyes widened. "The one's choosing the women's team for the trip to India?"

"And the men's team. Both have been invited to play. And what's really galling is that Excalibur was perfectly behaved and Felix scored three goals in that last match."

"I took some photos of you and Red. Here have a look." Sophia patted her pocket. "Where's my phone? I must have left it at the stables."

Sam filled the clubhouse entrance as he looked around. He spotted Rose and strode over to join her. "Your expression matches my mood," he remarked as he continued to observe the people gathered in the courtyard.

Rose realised her brow was wrinkled, and she'd clasped her hands in front of her.

Sam continued, "Something's amiss. I can feel it. But when I look around, everyone is chatting and they appear to be enjoying themselves. Keep your eye's open," he instructed as he turned and stalked back into the clubhouse.

Dickie approached Rose and said, "Whilst Marina and her team lay out afternoon tea, I thought we could unveil Craig's portrait."

Rose's mouth was dry as she croaked, "You don't expect me to say anything, do you?"

"Only if you want to. But you will remove the cover? I've already hung the painting on the clubhouse wall."

"Yes, of course," replied Rose with relief.

"Let me fetch my spare bell from the car so I can call people inside."

Dickie returned with a small hand bell which he rang to gain the crowd's attention.

"Ladies and gentleman, please join us in the clubhouse to commemorate a former treasurer, and long-standing member of the North Kenya Polo Club."

Dickie ushered Rose inside and she stood at the front, by the end of the bar. Thabiti leaned over and asked, "Have you had a busy day?"

"No, thankfully. I'm sure there'll be horses with cuts and bruises to see to this evening but, touch wood," she placed her hand on the cedar bar top, "there have been no major injuries or accidents."

Dickie rang the bell again. He stood behind the bar and called, "Silence, everyone. Welcome to Timau Polo Grounds for our first major tournament. We will continue to use the main polo club ground, but at some point in the future we envisage moving here on a permanent basis.

"To celebrate the unofficial opening, and commemorate the life of one of our most active members, Craig Hardie, who sadly passed away in June, I'd like to ask his widow Rose to unveil a portrait of him. I hope it will hang above the bar for many years to come."

Rose felt the heat rise to her cheeks as she walked behind the bar and stood next to Dickie.

Dickie pointed to the corner of a piece of kikoi material draped over the painting. "Gently tug here," he instructed, "and the kikoi should come away."

At first the material caught on a corner of the frame, but Dickie unhooked it and an image of a pensive Craig stared back at her. Tears pricked her eyes.

"Thank you," she whispered to Dickie, as those in the clubhouse clapped, cheered and raised a glass to toast Craig.

"And now, afternoon tea should be ready on the tables beside the door," Dickie announced.

Several men approached the bar.

"Are you OK?" whispered Thabiti.

Sam and Sergeant Wachira, who was not in uniform, pushed past Thabiti and took up positions behind the bar. They said in unison, to those waiting in front of it, "What can I get you?"

Rose sniffed and nodded at Thabiti. "I'll be fine. You better go and help. The bar's getting busy."

Several more people joined the queue, including the dark-featured Rufus who raised his hand, and his voice, as he challenged, "How long does it take to get a drink around here?"

"Aren't you playing in another match?" commented Poppy as she walked past him towards Rose.

Rufus ignored her.

Poppy said, "Come on, let's get a cup of tea and sit by the fireplace. It's too busy outside." She ushered Rose to some chairs and brought across two cups of tea and a plate of cakes and sandwiches to share.

"You looked rather startled when you unveiled Craig's portrait. Don't you like it?"

Rose sipped her tea before she answered. "The likeness is incredible. The painter has captured his introspective and appraising look perfectly. But it was such a shock, as if I could reach out and touch him."

"Dickie had a smaller painting commissioned for you. It's at home so don't forget to take it with you tomorrow."

Rose turned and looked back at Craig's portrait. "That's very kind of him. And now Craig can look down on the club members and listen to their conversations. Not that he'll recognise many of their voices. There are so few of us left."

"There's still you, me and Dickie. Poor Dora's been a widow for nearly twenty years, but Birdie and Terry are still going strong, and supporting their children and grandchildren."

Poppy nibbled on an egg and cress sandwich. "It's great welcoming new players, but I enjoy watching the children and grandchildren of those we knew, and who Dickie and Craig played against. The sport is still strong, and for that we should be thankful."

Rose looked at Craig's portrait again and smiled.

CHAPTER SIXTEEN

On Saturday evening, as the daylight began to fade, Rose walked with Poppy and Dickie Chambers from their house on Wild Dog Estate to the Timau Polo Grounds' clubhouse.

As they passed the stables, Rose spotted a group of syces sitting around a small campfire, chatting and drinking from plastic mugs.

From the stables there were the usual noises, such as the snort or whinny of a horse, or a clang as one of them nudged or leaned against one of the metal poles which divided the stables.

As they approached the clubhouse, Rose sniffed at the smell of roast meat hanging in the air from the BBQ. Poppy and Dickie excused themselves.

Thabiti carried a black plastic crate into which he deposited several empty Tusker beer bottles. He looked up, saw Rose, and carried the crate over, resting it on the wall beside her.

He said, "I can't believe how busy the bar's been and it's only half-past six. This could be a messy night. Luckily Marina and I are leaving now, but Judy and Sam are running the bar all evening."

They surveyed the crowd. Close to them, two smartly dressed African gentlemen and a European woman were huddled around a clipboard. Jasper Armitage approached and greeted each of them in turn.

"Well done for all your hard work umpiring today," said one of the men as he clasped Jasper's hand. "I'm so sorry you can't play this weekend. I was looking forward to your match against Felix Kamau. We will still take you into account for the upcoming trip to India, but the players with recent match experience will have priority."

Felix Kamau and Sophia stepped out of the clubhouse laughing. They spied Jasper and the selectors and strode across to them.

The second male selector looked up and said, "Well done, Felix. Fantastic play today."

Jasper crossed his arms over his chest.

"Thank you," replied Felix. "Can I introduce Sophia Gilbert, who's a member of the Only Fools on Horses team."

"Hi," said Sophia in a slightly breathless voice.

"It's nice to see younger players coming through, even if they are riding horses which are too advanced for them," the woman said in a clipped voice. "I would have thought Red was more suitable for you, Felix."

Sophia looked down at her clasped hands.

"I'm sure he would have bought him from under Sophia's nose if he'd had the chance," quipped Jasper, and he turned on his heels and stalked into the clubhouse.

Felix appeared to ignore the comment and instead responded, "Excalibur is an excellent horse and I'm very lucky. But Sophia and Red are a new combination and during the lessons I've given them this week, they've really improved."

Thabiti whispered to Rose, "There's trouble brewing there." He picked up his crate and added, "See you in the morning."

Poppy joined Rose and handed her a glass of white wine. "Dickie bought us a bottle, which Sam said he'd keep cool in the fridge for us. So, what's happening out here?"

Mr Gilbert looked earnest, with his head tilted to one side, as he spoke to Yaro and Jasmine Macharia. Sophia left the selectors and, with a despondent look, joined her father.

Mr Gilbert looked back at Felix and down at his daughter. He wrapped an arm around her shoulder and asked, "Is everything all right?"

"It's fine," she replied, and smiled weakly.

"You know Yaro, and his wife Jasmine, don't you?"

"Hi," muttered Sophia as she leaned against her father.

Poppy said to Rose. "You do love observing people, and I think I can see why. Oh dear, Jasmine Macharia is chasing after Felix again."

Jasmine left her group and intercepted Felix as he headed towards the rear of the courtyard. She smoothed her hair and leaned in closer to whisper in his ear.

She laughed at Felix's response.

"That's not good," remarked Poppy.

Rose followed her gaze, which was settled on Yaro. His gleaming teeth were bared and his eyes protruded, even behind his glasses. He marched up to Felix, grabbed Jasmine by the arm and jabbed a finger in Felix's face. "I've told you before. Stay away from my wife."

Felix shuffled his feet.

As Yaro led Jasmine away, she turned her head towards Felix, blew him a kiss and called, "See you later, sweetie." She was giggling as Yaro marched her into the clubhouse.

Later in the evening, Rose stood in the queue for the BBQ in the clubhouse courtyard with Poppy and Dickie.

A group of polo players, including Sophia, Felix and the fair-haired Otto, were sitting at a nearby picnic table. Jasper Armitage was talking to Mr Gilbert beside the entrance to the clubhouse.

Rose shivered and said, "I forget how much colder the nights are in Timau."

"We're another thousand feet above sea level from Nanyuki," explained Dickie. "I hope all the Nairobi players remembered to bring rugs to keep their horses warm. Most played two or three matches today."

Their conversation was interrupted when Jasper called out, "Watch it," as swarthy Rufus staggered out of the clubhouse and bumped into Mr Gilbert.

Rufus raised his bottle of beer in a dismissive gesture. Spotting the players at the picnic table, he called, "I see you're making yourself comfortable, Felix. First, you take my place on the Painted Dogs team, and now you're muscling in on my friends."

Felix pushed himself upright, but Otto, who was seated next to him, pulled him back down and said, "Rufus, the place was Jasper's, not yours. And are you surprised you weren't chosen to replace him? Look at the state of you. Besides, you've hardly been a team player today. You'd be better off concentrating on your own play rather than always criticising Sophia about hers."

"Get lost, the lot of you," slurred Rufus, and he wound his way across the courtyard and down the bank towards the polo pitches and stables.

Rose, Poppy and Dickie ate their supper inside the clubhouse, but by the time they'd finished, they were struggling to hear each other speak.

Poppy leaned forward and raised her voice as she said, "The more they drink, the louder the noise is in here."

"And the tension," muttered Rose, feeling uneasy.

"Why don't we go home for coffee," suggested Poppy.

"I'd better stay," replied Dickie. "I doubt anyone will mess with Sam, but it's not fair leaving him and Judy here without a senior member of the polo club. I wonder where Yaro is?"

Rose and Poppy crossed the main polo pitch, guided by the light of Poppy's torch. As they walked past the stables, they heard raised voices.

"Who do you think that is?" asked Rose. "They'll be upsetting the horses."

"I don't know, but let's not get involved. It's probably just a couple of syces who've had a little too much to drink, and are settling old scores."

They walked on to a small wooden gate set in the fence which separated the polo ground from Wild Dog Estate.

As Rose closed the gate and looked back, a figure slunk down a row of stables. She hoped Gathi wouldn't cause Chumba any more trouble.

CHAPTER SEVENTEEN

O n Sunday morning, Rose and Poppy Chambers were enjoying early morning cups of tea on Poppy's veranda, which had been built facing Mount Kenya.

Rose was admiring the view of the mountain she remembered from when she had lived nearby on a farm Craig managed. Rather than a single peak, which was visible from Nanyuki, the three primary peaks stood out clearly against the pale blue sky.

"I'm pleased to see snow on the mountain. I hope it means there'll be rain in the near future," commented Rose. "We certainly need it."

Poppy sipped her tea and replied, "We had some showers in July, which were most welcome. They filled our water tanks and gave the grass and flowers a boost."

She glanced back into the house. "I hope you don't mind waiting for breakfast, but Dickie wanted to check his emails."

"I'm enjoying the peace out here, as I expect we'll have another busy day. I didn't hear Dickie come in last night. Was he late back?" asked Rose.

"No, he arrived home before midnight. Apparently, there'd been several scuffles, and I think a few punches were thrown. He and Sam agreed to shut the bar early and send everyone home."

"Very sensible. Especially as many of them are playing today."

Poppy shrugged. "They're young and most can handle it. But a hungover Rufus in an ugly mood, and in charge of a polo stick, could be dangerous."

Rose thought she heard a gate creak, and moments later Chumba ran around the corner.

He stood at the bottom of the veranda steps, wide-eyed and panting slightly. "Bwana Chambers. Where is Bwana Chambers?"

Dickie must have heard the call as he stepped out onto the veranda, rubbing his glasses with his green paisley handkerchief. "Did someone call?"

Chumba ran up the steps two at a time and grabbed Dickie's sleeve. "Come quick. Master Felix is asleep and I not wake him."

"Now steady on," said Dickie, stepping back.

Rose said calmly, "Chumba, when you say you can't wake him, what do you mean? Where is he sleeping?" Rose felt her chest tightening as she waited for his answer.

"In pretty horse stable of Miss Sophia."

"Felix is lying on the floor of Red's stable," stated Poppy perceptively.

Rose, Poppy and Dickie exchanged worried glances.

Dickie announced, "Wait here young man, I'll fetch my jacket."

"I'll come with you," added Rose, "but first …"

She picked up her phone from beside her teacup.

"Habari, Mama Rose," said a sleepy sounding Sam, who picked up after several rings.

"So sorry to disturb you, but are you and Sergeant, Judy, staying near the polo ground?"

Sam sounded more alert as he replied, "We're camping here. Why, what's happened?"

"Chumba's arrived at the Chambers' house and he says Felix Kamau is asleep in one of the stables, and he can't wake him."

"Oh," replied Sam. "And are you concerned he's injured, or worse, but can't say so in front of Chumba?"

"Exactly." Rose glanced across at Chumba's flushed, innocent face.

Dickie walked back onto the veranda. "Lead the way," he instructed Chumba.

"Sam, we're heading to the stables now. I'll meet you and Sergeant Wachira there."

Chumba and the quick-striding Dickie reached the stables before Rose. Chumba was struggling to pull on Red's headcollar when she arrived. Red's nostrils flared, and he stamped his hooves impatiently.

"Let me help," instructed Dickie. He swiftly pulled the strap over the top of the horse's head and buckled it securely. Chumba led Red out and Dickie said, "Take him for a walk and let him nibble some grass."

Rose and Dickie watched Chumba lead Red away, before Dickie declared, "Now the horse and boy are out of the way, we'd better attend to the matter in hand."

Rose looked into the stable. Felix was lying in the far left corner, on his back, but slightly hunched over. She couldn't see his face.

Dickie was about to step over the bottom entrance pole, but Rose put an arm out to restrain him.

"I think I might be better doing this. It's likely to be a police matter and in the absence of a doctor, I can give my medical opinion."

"You think he's dead?"

"Don't you?"

Dickie nodded his head slowly, and Rose thought he looked all of his seventy plus years.

She stepped over the entrance pole and squatted beside Felix. She touched him and her blood felt as chilled as his body.

She stood up, "Yes, he's dead, and from the temperature of his body, and the fact that it's already stiff, I'd say he's been lying here all night."

CHAPTER EIGHTEEN

G roups of syces had gathered at either end of the stable block and Rose thought she spotted Gathi hiding amongst them.

An unshaven Sam and a sleepy-looking Sergeant Wachira pushed past one group and joined Rose and Dickie outside Red's stable.

"What have we got?" asked Sam.

Rose stepped aside so he and Sergeant Wachira had a clear view inside the stable. She said, "He's definitely dead, and rigor mortis has set in."

"Which means he died last night," deduced Sergeant Wachira, whose eyes were now focused and bright. "Have you examined him?"

"No, I wanted to wait for you."

"Thank you." Sergeant Wachira's voice was clear and authoritative as she asked, "Mr Chambers, would you mind dispersing the onlookers."

Rose entered the stable again, followed by Sergeant Wachira, and squatted beside Felix. Sam watched from the entrance.

"Can you help me roll him over?" Rose asked the young sergeant. As they did, a gash on his forehead, with dried blood, was immediately visible.

"Could that have killed him?" asked the sergeant.

"Perhaps," considered Rose, biting her lip. "There's also a tear in his trousers, so there may be other marks." Rose surveyed the body. "Would you object if I lifted his shirt?"

Rose pulled up Felix's shirt, with the help of Sergeant Wachira, and then sat back on her heels.

There was a large bruise on Felix's chest and in the centre the semi-circular outline of a horse's hoof. "As I suspected," pronounced Rose, "he's been kicked by Red, and this is likely to have been the fatal wound. I presume the family will allow an autopsy?"

"We'll certainly try to persuade them," replied the Sergeant. "Do you have any other thoughts on his death?"

Rose stood and half-turned towards Sam. "I recently read an article in an English horse magazine. A 68-year-old man was kicked in the chest by his horse and died. The blow ruptured the pericardium, which is a thin, double-walled sac that surrounds the heart. The wall cavity filled with blood and compressed the heart to such an extent that it couldn't pump enough blood around his body. The man went into shock and died. I suspect something similar has occurred here."

They were interrupted by Sophia's arrival. "What's happened? Why are you in my stable?

Is it Red? Has something happened to him?" Sophia's eyes bulged.

Dickie returned and stood beside Sophia.

Rose was unsure if it was Red or Chumba who had heard Sophia's cry as the horse rounded the corner of the stable block towing Chumba.

Sophia ran towards her horse and wrapped her arms around his neck. "Thank you, Chumba. Was he annoyed that I'm late feeding him?"

Chumba said nothing, but gave Rose an appealing look.

The business-like Sergeant Wachira approached Sophia. "I'm afraid there's been an accident. Felix Kamau has been found dead in your horse's stable."

"Felix. No. That's not possible. I was with him last night at the party. He can't be dead. Anyway, why would he be in Red's stable?"

"I hoped you might be able to tell us that," pressed the newly appointed sergeant.

"You're not joking, are you?" Sophia's flushed face turned white.

Rose joined the two women and asked, "Do you mind if I check Red over? Just to make sure he hasn't injured himself," she assured Sophia, but glanced back at Sergeant Wachira, who nodded her consent.

Sophia seemed frozen in place.

"There are some cuts on his legs, and one on his shoulder, but nothing serious. I've some ointment to help those heal." Rose patted Red's neck, but he flinched. "You can still play him today but be careful, he might be more flighty than usual."

Behind them, Excalibur used his front foot to paw the ground.

"Chumba, can you feed Felix's ponies?" Rose asked.

Chumba turned and ran towards the storeroom.

Sophia reached for Red's lead rope. Rose put a hand on the girl's arm and said softly, "You'll have to find another stable. I'm afraid he can't go back in his, it's a crime scene now."

Tears welled up in Sophia's eyes as she turned, stumbled, and led her horse away.

Outside Felix's storeroom, she bumped into Jasper Armitage, who asked, "Are you OK? Someone said Felix had an accident down at the stables."

Sophia sniffed and leaned against her horse. "Jasper, he's dead. And they found him in Red's stable." She almost lost her balance as Red lurched forward and tried to poke his head into a bucket Chumba carried out of the storeroom.

"Let's settle Red first and give him a feed. There's a spare stable next to Boadicea." Jasper took hold of the lead rope with one hand, and wrapped the other around Sophia's shoulders, and led them both away.

Rose returned to Red's stable. Dickie had found a tarpaulin, which he handed to Sam, who laid it over Felix's body.

Sergeant Wachira was speaking into her phone. "Yes, Commissioner. I'll wait here until the ambulance arrives from the Cottage Hospital." She listened, and then said, "His parents were at the tournament yesterday. I think someone said they were staying at the Mount Kenya Resort and Spa."

There was a further pause. "Thank you. I would be grateful if you could deal with them while I sort out the body and start proceedings here. I don't see any reason to stop the tournament though, if the polo club wants it to go ahead."

She looked across at Dickie, who nodded his head and closed his eyes.

Sergeant Wachira finished her call. "Mr Chambers, we see no reason why today's matches can't go ahead as planned." The sergeant's tone was matter of fact.

"Thank you," replied Dickie. "And the police are contacting Felix's parents?"

"Commissioner Akida will see to it personally."

Dickie looked down at his feet and shook his head. "This will not help our relationship with the government, and the African community. And Felix was such a bright boy, and an excellent player. He'll be sorely missed." Dickie turned and trudged towards the main pitch and the clubhouse.

CHAPTER NINETEEN

R ose, Sam and Sergeant Wachira stood beside the entrance to Red's stable. Felix's body was covered by a tarpaulin. The syces' initial interest had waned and work needed to be done feeding and preparing the polo ponies for the day's matches.

Rose leant down and picked up an empty crisp packet, which she folded and stuffed in her pocket.

Sergeant Wachira gazed over the top of the rows of stables at the bustle of activity and said, "I have two initial questions. First, why would a horse kick Felix? And so violently? Looking around, I can see the syces going in and out of stables, yet the horses are relaxed, and are not trying to kill them. And second, why was Felix in Sophia's horse's stable and not one of his own horses?"

Rose looked over the top of the adjacent row of stables but she could not see Red, and presumed his head was pushed into a bucket as he ate his breakfast.

She replied, "I can answer both questions, but in purely theoretical terms as I've no idea what actually took place. Throughout evolution, the horse's survival has depended on its ability to flee from danger. This is true of many mammals, such as an impala attempting to escape a pack of chasing African wild dogs. But unlike impala, a horse has a powerful kick and will resort to fighting to protect itself if it is unable to flee."

Chumba approached, balancing three buckets in his arms. He deposited them on the floor of the three adjacent stables, which were still occupied by Sophia's other polo ponies.

The horses immediately thrust their heads into the buckets, and munching and crunching noises permeated the air.

As Chumba retreated back to Felix's storeroom, Rose continued, "Why would Felix go into Red's stable? Well, he might have noticed that the horse was anxious after yesterday's matches, or his rug might have been askew and he wanted to right it, or Red might have been lying down and struggling to get up, which we term as cast. Most horsey people will attend to someone else's horse if it's in trouble, or if something is amiss."

Sam was leaning over the entrance rail of a stable, watching the horse inside eat. Without looking up, he stated, "So it's not unusual for a person to be kicked and die."

"It is rare," replied Rose.

"Horses are not naturally aggressive creatures, but it does happen. Particularly if the person is standing behind the horse and something shocks or surprises it, like a loud noise from a public address system at an event. And Red was in a confined space so would not be able to flee if he was scared."

Sam stood and looked around.

"It's a shame our witnesses can't provide some of the answers."

"The horses certainly can't, and the syces will be as tight-lipped as their charges. They're unlikely to volunteer information," Rose conceded.

Sergeant Wachira tapped the top of a pole and pondered, "So what are we looking at? A tragic accident or something more sinister?"

The hairs lifted on the back of Rose's neck.

"I'm not sure. We need to establish why Felix was down at the stables last night, and if he was alone or with someone else."

CHAPTER TWENTY

R ose left Sam and Sergeant Wachira at the stables and wandered across the main polo pitch towards the clubhouse. Despite having slept well, she felt weary as she climbed the bank to the clubhouse.

Poppy had her back to Rose and was organising cups and vacuum flasks on a white, cloth-covered table. Next to it was another table on which a squat, 3kg LPG gas bottle was positioned.

Thabiti appeared carrying a cooking ring and burner which he began to attach to the top of the gas bottle. Marina carried a large round insulated casserole pot and the smell of bacon immediately roused the group of subdued polo players slumped over a nearby picnic table.

Sophia and Jasper must have followed Rose as they joined the polo players and began a whispered discussion. Sophia's eyes were red-rimmed and Jasper had a set expression.

Rose walked across the courtyard and joined Marina.

Thabiti lit the burner on top of the gas bottle, and said, "All set, you can start frying eggs, and if you need someone to test the first one, I'm a willing volunteer."

He turned towards Rose. "Habari, Mama Rose. We have bacon rolls for two hundred and fifty shillings or egg and bacon rolls for three hundred and fifty shillings."

"The smell of bacon is very tempting, but I think I'll start with a cup of tea," Rose replied and looked across to the adjacent white-clothed table.

"Drinks are complimentary," Thabiti informed her. He lowered his voice, "But the breakfast rolls are our own venture, so hopefully we can make a small profit."

Marina grinned and added, "The first for our shop and cafe business."

Thabiti looked around and commented, "It must have been a riotous party last night. Everyone is very quiet and withdrawn this morning. And have you seen Sam and Judy? I thought they were having a lie-in, but I checked their tent and it's empty."

Rose glanced from left to right and leaned closer to Thabiti and Marina. "They're down at the stables. Chumba discovered one of the polo players this morning who he thought was asleep, but he was actually dead."

There was a clatter as the frying pan Marina was lifting fell back to the table. "What?" she gasped.

"Is it a suspicious death?" asked Thabiti. "Or should I already know the answer to that question?"

"It looks like the polo player, Felix Kamau, received a fatal kick from a horse, but it's not apparent why he was near the horse or what provoked it to kick him."

A silver Nissan X-Trail drew up and parked by the entrance to the courtyard. Otto Wakeman climbed out flicking his long fair curls away from his face. He pulled what looked like a wheelchair out of the back of the car.

Poppy carried another vacuum flask across to the drinks table, and Rose joined her.

"This is terrible," murmured Poppy as she placed the flask on the table. "Dickie is trying to be stoic and reorganise today's tournament, but I can tell Felix's death has shaken him. It was an accident, wasn't it?" Poppy pleaded.

Rose laid a hand on her arm, "I'm sure it was, but the police will have to conduct a thorough investigation, especially as Felix's family is so well connected."

Poppy handed Rose a cup of tea and they both turned back to face the courtyard. Otto was pushing an old man with wispy grey hair towards the table of polo players. He parked the wheelchair at one end and said to the silent group, "I've brought Granddad for an outing and some fresh air."

Most of the players continued to lie with their heads resting on their arms on the table and, although a few looked up, nobody responded.

"Well, I'm not sure I should have bothered. You'd think someone had died."

Sophia squawked and buried her head in Jasper's chest.

The colour drained from Otto's face.

Jasper looked across at Otto and muttered, "Felix is dead."

Rose and Poppy carried their drinks towards an empty table. As Rose passed the polo players, the old man, who had been slumped in his wheelchair, raised his head and stared straight into her eyes. "Carrie," he cried. "But I thought you were dead." He sounded confused.

"I'm sorry," apologised Otto, whose pale face matched the colour of his hair. With shaking hands, he settled his grandfather, and said, "He's increasingly talking about people and events from his past, but has no idea who I am."

Poppy led Rose to a table and said, "I remember Harold Wakeman, the man in the wheelchair, when he was a young man, as he used to visit my parents. But I think something happened, and he moved to Zambia. I heard he found a job in a copper mine and married a girl there. His wife died recently so the family have moved him to the Louise Decker Centre, at the cottage hospital."

Dickie sat down next to them and slammed his cup of coffee on the table. It slopped dangerously from side to side, but did not spill.

"I've no idea what to do," Dickie said dejectedly. "Despite having confirmation from the police that we can continue with the tournament today, I'm not sure we can without one of our key players. The Painted Dogs are in the quarter-finals, and I had expected them to win the cup."

A deep, throaty mechanical noise broke the hushed morning air and an old battered Land Rover Defender pulled up next to Otto's silver X-Trail. Rufus, looking even more swarthy and unkempt than usual, slid out and slunk towards the group of polo players.

He took a long slurp from a can of Coke and wiped his mouth with the back of his hand. "Is it true?" he demanded. "Is Felix dead?"

"Is that necessary?" rebuked Jasper. But in a softer tone he added, "Yes, Felix's body was found down at the stables."

Sophia sniffled and covered her eyes with her hand.

"Who's taking his place on the Painted Dogs team then?" Rufus's eyes surveyed the group.

"How should we know?" implored Jasper. "It's hardly been top of our thoughts."

"Well, it's been top of mine." Rufus sat down heavily on the bench of the neighbouring table, facing outwards, towards the group of players. "I think I should take Felix's place. It should have been mine to start with." He sat up and thrust out his chest.

"I don't think I want to play today," muttered Sophia.

"Then Jasper could borrow Red and take Felix's place back on the Painted Dogs team," suggested Otto.

"That's hardly fair, and the Only Fools on Horses team will be a player short," remarked Jasper.

"So? Only Fools on Horses scraped into the quarterfinals, but the Painted Dogs have a real chance of winning," added Rufus loudly.

"But that's hardly the point," remonstrated Jasper. "Sophia, I think you need to play today, to concentrate on something besides this morning's events."

Sophie looked at him with large, pleading eyes.

"You don't want to ride Red, is that it?"

Sophia nodded.

"Because you think he could have killed Felix?"

Sophia chewed her thumb.

"Even if he did, it's not Red's fault," Jasper sympathised.

"I know," Sophia said in a small voice. "But I'm worried about riding him today."

"Would you feel better if I rode him and you borrowed Biscuit?"

Sophia looked relieved and nodded again.

"I know," pressed Otto. "Jasper, why don't you borrow Excalibur and Red, and play on the Painted Dogs Team."

"Now just a minute," thundered Rufus. "I hardly think Felix would want you borrowing

Excalibur. Not after the way you lambasted him for buying the horse from under your nose."

Otto looked thoughtful. "But Felix wouldn't mind Sophia riding him." He leaned towards Sophia. "Didn't he give you a lesson on Excalibur?"

"Yes," whispered Sophia.

"So," concluded Otto, "Jasper can rejoin the Painted Dogs with Red, Biscuit and Storm. And if you need a fourth pony, you can borrow one of mine, and Sophia can ride Excalibur."

"Excellent," conceded Dickie, as he turned back to face Rose and Poppy. They had been following the player's discussion with interest. "We can go ahead with the tournament as planned. Excuse me, I need to organise some black armbands."

Dickie strode away as Rufus jumped and up and shouted, "I don't believe it. After all that effort and you still won't let me play for the Painted Dogs."

CHAPTER TWENTY-ONE

Thabiti bit into his bacon and fried egg roll and tried to follow the events happening around him.

The dark-featured polo player, Rufus, who he now remembered from school, and who'd been well on the way to getting drunk when he and Marina had left yesterday evening, was irritating the other players.

Mama Rose approached him and said, "I'm going back to the Chambers' house to pack my things, and Poppy has organised breakfast for us."

She gave him and Marina an apologetic look. "Can you tell Sam and Sergeant Wachira that'll I'll be back in an hour or two?"

Rose left the courtyard with Mrs Chambers and they chatted briefly with Sam and Judy, who they met walking up the bank.

Rufus's dark features looked menacing as he climbed into his dilapidated Land Rover and revved the engine. The car shot forward, nearly knocking over Mr Gilbert, who jumped out of its way.

Mr Gilbert, who wore an elegant navy linen jacket, approached the polo players and asked, "Does anyone here own a black Amazon Land Cruiser? There's one in the car park which is all steamed up and it looks as if someone is inside. I presume they're just sleeping but …?"

Sam and Judy marched across to Mr Gilbert, and Judy said in an authoritative tone, "We'll take a look."

Thabiti shoved the last piece of roll into his mouth, wiped his hands with a napkin and rushed after them.

A temporary car parking area had been marked out with wooden poles and red-and-white plastic tape. Only a few cars were currently parked in it so the large black Land Cruiser, with its fogged windows, was obvious.

Sam and Judy approached the car purposefully and stared through its windows. As Thabiti reached them, he heard Sam report, "There's a man in here. I think he was the one with the attractive wife who kept flirting with our victim last night."

Thabiti said excitedly, "Do you think his wife is a black widow serial killer? And she killed both her lover and her husband."

Judy gave him a withering look, and he snapped his mouth shut.

Sam tried the door handle, and the catch clicked open. As he pulled the door ajar, the figure in the front passenger seat slowly opened his eyes and looked around in confusion. Thabiti recognised Yaro Macharia, even without his black-rimmed glasses, and he sported a large black eye.

Yaro coughed and asked in a hoarse voice, "What time is it?"

"Nearly nine o'clock," answered Judy. "Did you sleep in you car all night?"

Yaro shuffled and hoisted himself upright using the grab handle. The seat had been lowered flat to sleep on. He looked into the rear of the car and then at Judy. "Jasmine. Where is Jasmine?"

Judy looked towards Thabiti, who shrugged and replied, "She's not been at the clubhouse this morning."

"Mr Macharia, when did you last see your wife?" Judy pressed.

"I'm not sure, I don't remember. In fact, I don't remember much about last night."

"Do you know how you got that black eye?" asked Sam.

"What black eye?"

As Thabiti returned from the car park, he saw Marina struggling to make breakfast rolls whilst simultaneously frying eggs.

The smell of bacon must have roused the polo players who now stood in a line in front of Marina so Thabiti rushed across to help her.

"We've budgeted for two slices of bacon per roll," instructed Marina.

Mr Gilbert walked past and approached his daughter, Sophia. He sniffed the air and said, "I'd love to buy you breakfast Soph, but I've misplaced my wallet."

"Like my phone then," she replied in a lacklustre manner. "Thanks, Dad, but I'm not hungry."

She reached into a pocket of her white polo breeches and held up a thousand shilling note. "But you must be starving. Grab yourself a roll, and you don't need to pay for tea and coffee."

Mr Gilbert joined the dwindling queue and requested, "A bacon sandwich, please."

As the initial rush had subsided, Thabiti helped himself to a second bacon roll and joined Sam.

Judy walked out of the clubhouse and sat with them.

She said, "The last thing Mr Macharia can remember about last night is eating supper from the BBQ, which he thinks was around half-past nine. He has no idea where his wife is, and she's not answering her phone. If we don't find her soon, I'll have to start a search of the polo grounds." Judy's face and neck were tense.

Sam mused, "And we thought this would be a quiet weekend of bar duty, not one where we were examining dead bodies and searching for missing people."

Judy pursed her lips and said, "It's certainly not what I was expecting of my first weekend at a polo tournament. Mr Chambers has taken Mr Macharia back to his house on Wild Dog Estate to freshen up."

Marina approached and handed breakfast rolls to Sam and Judy. "Tea or coffee?" she enquired.

"Thanks, that's just what I need," replied Judy, "And I'd love a cup of tea, with two sugars to energise me."

"Coffee, for me please," responded Sam.

"And me," added Thabiti.

Marina raised her eyebrows, and Thabiti quickly looked down at the table.

Judy opened a notebook and asked, "Just who was Felix Kamau? We need to find someone who knew him."

Thabiti looked up and said, "I was at school with him. That is, he was older than me and after two years he left to attend a smart English school. Did you hear how he spoke?"

Judy shook her head, "No, I didn't speak to him."

Sam placed his partially eaten roll on a paper plate and disclosed, "I did, and he was very polite. His accent was crisp, and like that of the British upper classes in movies."

"Exactly," agreed Thabiti. "He was well educated and equally well connected. Ma didn't share the same political affinities as his father, who I know was part of a group she distrusted. The ones whose wealth and power increases in proportion with their time in office."

Judy confirmed, "And according to the Commissioner his father is still a politician."

Sam mused, "So he would have enemies. But was his son, Felix, interested in politics?"

Thabiti shrugged, "I've no idea."

Judy scribbled in her notebook and explained, "I'll ask his polo colleagues. And I need to find out where he lived, and where he was supposed to be sleeping last night. His parents are staying at the Mount Kenya Resort and Spa."

CHAPTER TWENTY-TWO

Rose still felt unsettled during breakfast with Poppy Chambers at her house on Wild Dog Estate. She quickly packed her overnight bag and asked, "Do you mind if I go to church?"

"Not at all," Poppy replied, "but what shall I tell Dickie?"

"That I'll be back at the polo club in an hour, an hour and a half at the latest."

Rose drove along the highway, which cut through the middle of Timau, a small dusty town. Most of the shops were closed but several groups of people, dressed in brightly coloured dresses and ill-fitting suits, walked along the dirt tracks towards their denomination of church.

Rose turned right at the southern end of the town into a white-walled complex whose buildings included a church, a small hospital, and accommodation for the priest and three nuns.

Several cars were parked next to the church and she heard singing inside. Silently, she entered the church and sat alone in a pew near the back. With her head bowed, she allowed the priest's prayers to comfort her.

She tried to think of poor Felix Kamau, but instead her thoughts were drawn back to the sad figure of Otto Wakeman's grandfather.

She knew she was getting older but since Craig's death, she'd caught fleeting threads of dreams about her childhood. Her memories of her mother were vague, and her father had refused to talk about her, and particularly her death, which had been due to an accident of some sort.

Her father ensured that her brother had an education, both formal and in the workings of the farm, and sent him away to boarding school less than two years after their mother's death.

Rose recollected the wonderful time she spent with her brother when he was home from school, but outside his school holidays, Rose was left to occupy herself. She joined the village children, and those whose parents worked on her father's farm, at the local school where she learnt the basics of English and maths.

Her mother had filled many bookshelves which her father left untouched, so Rose had slowly worked her way through the classics. But the books that really touched her were Doris Lessing's *The Grass is Singing*, and J.D. Salinger's *The Catcher in the Rye*.

She still had her mother's copies of both books, which were tattered and torn from the countless times she'd reread them over the years. *The Catcher in the Rye* had particularly affected her after her father finally bowed to the pressure of local European farmers' wives, and sent her away to boarding school in Nairobi.

She wasn't especially academic and spent most of her time gazing out of the open classroom windows at the parched grass playing fields. It was on them that she truly excelled. She smiled to herself. If it hadn't been for Thabiti's mother, Aisha, she would never have passed her end-of-year exams.

She was aware of the small congregation filing past as the service ended, but her head remained bowed. Father Donald sat down next to her with only the swish of his vestments to indicate his presence. They remained sitting in silence for several minutes.

Finally, Rose lifted her head and sat back in the pew.

"Rose, I'm delighted to welcome you back into our church and please accept my condolences for Craig's passing. Is that what troubles you?"

Rose stared at the gold cross standing proudly on the altar at the front of the church, and replied, "I do miss Craig, but he would only have suffered further pain and frustration. I know his death was a blessing, even if I don't always find that easy to remember. But today I needed solace in the peace of your church.

Terrible things keep happening and I'm not sure I have the strength to the make them right."

Father Donald's tone was comforting as he said, "I am always here to guide and reassure you on your journey."

CHAPTER TWENTY-THREE

As Rose parked in the taped-off area near the clubhouse, she spotted the diminutive stature of Sergeant Wachira beside Sam's towering figure, as they walked towards her from the boundary of the polo ground.

"Having a stroll to clear your heads?" Rose enquired.

Sergeant Wachira stopped beside Rose's Land Rover and replied, "No, we've been looking for Jasmine Macharia, who's still not answering her phone."

Sam added, "And we've checked the stables, the area around the clubhouse, and the campsite, but there's no sign of her."

Sergeant Wachira leaned against the car. "I suppose I'll have to go for a run around the perimeter of the polo grounds. There's a whole area where hollows have been dug out to provide material for the entrance road. But first I need a cup of tea."

The young sergeant pushed herself away from Rose's car and strode towards the clubhouse. Sam and Rose followed her.

"When did you last see Felix?" Rose asked Sam as they entered the courtyard.

"I'm not sure. I don't think he was around at the end of the party when I had to break up yet another fight and Dickie closed the bar."

They helped themselves to tea and coffee and joined Sergeant Wachira at one of the picnic tables.

Sam sat down and asked the young sergeant, "When did you last see Felix?"

"It wasn't late. The elusive Jasmine Macharia had him pinned in a corner, and angry words were exchanged as Mr Macharia dragged his wife away."

Rose recalled the previous evening. "Poppy and I heard someone having a row down at the stables when we walked back to Wild Dog Estate."

"When was that?" Sergeant Wachira asked sharply.

"Nine thirty, quarter to ten."

"Did you recognise the voices, or see anyone?"

Rose cradled her tea. "The voices no, but I thought I spotted Gathi skulking in the shadows."

"Who's Gathi?" Sergeant Wachira looked perplexed.

Sam's eyes narrowed. "Wasn't he bothering Chumba yesterday? And trying to interfere with Felix's polo ponies?"

Rose sipped her tea and returned her cup to the table. "He's a troublesome syce with a well-placed reputation for drinking. He's worked for most of the horsey people in Nairobi, and I think he's been trying to find work up here after Felix sacked him."

Sergeant Wachira sat up and her eyes were bright. "That's an excellent motive for wanting to harm Felix, even kill him. And he'd know all about the behaviour of horses. Where can we find this Gathi?"

Rose remained at the picnic table while Sam and Sergeant Wachira strode purposely towards the stables in search of Gathi.

A Subaru pulled up beside the entrance to the courtyard and Yaro Macharia and Dickie Chambers got out. From the back of the car, Dickie handed Yaro a cardboard box. He picked up two reed kikapu baskets, and they walked towards the clubhouse.

Dickie stopped beside Rose's table and rested his baskets on it. The gold lid of a tankard glittered in one. Dickie asked, "Have you decided what you'd like to award Craig's memorial trophy for?"

Rose leaned back and clasped her hands in front of her. "I still feel it shouldn't be for the best player, team or pony. But along the lines of the most improved, or for a player who has overcome adversity. Something like that."

Dickie lifted the gold tankard out of the kikapu and turned it around as he admired it.

"I remember when this was presented to Craig. It was the first tournament he played in. Because of his childhood polio, and the damage it did to his leg, nobody thought he would be able to ride a horse, never mind play polo against the best in the country. So you're right, it would be fitting to present it to a player who has shown particular strength, or courage, or overcome a challenge. I'll keep the exact wording for the award vague, but can I ask you to choose this year's recipient?"

Yaro joined them and asked, "Has anyone seen Jasmine? She's not answering her phone and I've no idea where she is."

Rose looked up at him. "Sergeant Wachira and Sam have been looking for her."

"I'll call some of our friends and see if she stayed with them." Yaro returned to the clubhouse. Dickie picked up his kikapus and followed him.

Rose was relieved to have some time to herself, but after five minutes, Sam and Sergeant Wachira rejoined her with a reluctant Gathi.

His grubby t-shirt was ripped and there was either blood or dirt covering the left knee of his ragged trousers. His eyes were shrunken and bloodshot.

Gathi looked at Rose's nearly empty cup and announced, "I want some tea."

Sam stood and wandered over to the drinks table. He returned with a mug of tea, which Gathi drank greedily. He held his empty cup up to Sam and demanded, "More."

Sam's jaw clenched, but he took the cup and returned to the drinks table.

Gathi sniffed the air, and announced, "I'm hungry."

"Then you can have some breakfast after we've finished interviewing you," responded Sergeant Wachira with a pinched expression. "How long did you work for Felix Kamau?"

"Couple of months," replied Gathi in a surly tone, as he grabbed his refilled cup from Sam.

"And why did he let you go?" pressed the young sergeant.

"It wasn't fair. I'd done nothing wrong."

Rose coughed. "As I recollect, you were drunk and had fallen asleep when you were supposed to be preparing Felix's ponies for last Sunday's matches."

Gathi gave Rose a sour look. "I would have done them."

"Were you angry with Felix for treating you badly?" continued Sergeant Wachira.

Gathi puffed out his chest. "Yeah, I was. He should have given me more respect."

Sam guffawed, and Gathi quickly looked down at his hands.

"And did you make your dissatisfaction known to him last night?" asked the sergeant.

Gathi shrugged. "Might have. Last night. Last week. I pleaded with him to give me my job back, but he refused. Instead, he employed some snivelling child." Gathi's eyes narrowed as he sneered at Rose.

"So you were angry with him last night. Did you have a row? Did Felix go into Sophia Gilbert's stable, and did you frighten her horse so it kicked him?"

Gathi's mouth fell open, and he sat rigidly still.

The others waited for his response.

As if the implications of the interview had finally hit him, Gathi spluttered, "I had nothing to do with this death. I didn't lure him into Red's stable. I didn't actually speak to him last night. I'm not the one he was having a row with."

Sergeant Wachira leaned forward and asked, "So, who was?"

Gathi looked around furtively and replied, with a smirk on his face, "Rufus."

CHAPTER TWENTY-FOUR

S ergeant Wachira let Gathi leave, but before he headed back towards the stables, he turned around and Rose caught a wild look in his eyes, and an unkind smirk of satisfaction. She knew he would only add to their troubles this morning.

Thabiti sat down at the picnic table and asked Sam, "Did you agree a time for opening the bar with bwana Chambers? And we'll need to restock it first, and put some beers in the fridge."

Dickie stepped out of the clubhouse with a piece of paper in each hand and a perplexed expression on his face.

"Which joker swapped my team sheets and score cards for these?" He waved the papers. "I'm sure we don't have any teams called 'The Tricky Dickies' or 'Jasper's Jolly Green Giants'."

Rose covered her mouth with her hand to hide her grin, but it would not be funny if the real sheets were not returned soon.

"That's just the sort of prank Rufus Esposito would play," Thabiti muttered. He started. "But how would I know that?"

They all looked at him, and Rose could sense the heat rising in his face as his ears turned pink. He looked down and uttered, "Oh, yes. I forgot."

"What did you forget?" pressed Sergeant Wachira.

"Do I have to tell you?" pleaded Thabiti.

Rose leaned towards him and said in a sympathetic tone. "It might help clear up some of the inconsistencies surrounding Felix's death. I take it something embarrassing happened."

Thabiti nodded. He took a deep breath, looked up and blurted, "He stole my school shorts."

Sam grinned, "And I presume you were standing in your pants, with all the other children laughing and pointing."

Thabiti hastily looked down and started pulling at the hem of his shorts.

"It was so embarrassing. I'd only been at school a few weeks and had no idea who to ask for help. Rufus was older than me and had a strong following and he could lead and bend the other pupils to his will. Some of the older ones stood up to him, like Felix Kamau. He was the one who rescued me."

Thabiti sat up, drew his lips together and gazed at the trees on the horizon. In a small voice he said, "I'd forgotten all about that, and I never had the chance to thank Felix properly."

"What other mischief did Rufus get up to?" enquired Dickie in a stern tone.

"Oh, he stole the school bell, removed the hoops from the basketball court and painted a second finishing line on the athletics track. That was quite funny and caused all sorts of confusion on sports day. But it all stopped when a pupil was seriously injured and ended up in hospital."

"It usually escalates until there is a tragedy," noted Rose.

"There was a narrow walled path leading to one of the school entrance gates. Rufus and some friends were at the front and started walking really slowly but other pupils, who knew they would be late for lessons, started pushing past each other, and a boy in the year above me fell down and was trampled."

"And that put an end to Rufus' pranks," pronounced Dickie.

"I think so," replied Thabiti slowly. "I'm sure Rufus was away from school for a few days and when he returned, he had a cut lip and a black eye. I remember because he joked about it and pretended he'd been in an amateur boxing match, but his eyes betrayed him."

There was silence for several minutes until Rose asked, "Can you remember anything about the relationship between Rufus and Felix?"

"Rufus resented Felix." Thabiti rubbed his chin. "But why?" He leaned back and looked up as three tan and brown Egyptian Geese flew over.

"I didn't understand as a child, but I think I can now. Felix had everything. He was from a wealthy family with an influential, and politically important, father. He was kind to the other children and popular. An all-round model pupil. But I think Rufus had issues at home. On more than one occasion, he came to school with injuries. I remember he once had his arm in a sling. Both he and Felix were on all the school teams, but I think Rufus had to work hard, whilst Felix found life much easier."

Sergeant Wachira stopped scribbling in her notebook and asked, "So there was a history of resentment between Rufus Esposito and Felix Kamau?"

Thabiti placed his hands on the table. "From Rufus, I guess, but I doubt Felix felt any animosity towards Rufus. Why should he?"

"You mean Felix had everything he wanted," suggested Rose.

"Exactly," replied Thabiti, and his shoulders slumped as he smiled sadly.

Dickie coughed. "That's all very interesting, but where are my sheets?"

Sam looked around and remarked, "I could take a look in Rufus's Land Rover. I doubt he's locked it as who would want to steal it?"

"Is that ethical or legal?" asked Dickie in a concerned tone.

Sergeant Wachira looked at her watch and stood up. "Perhaps not, but I understand the first match is at half past ten, which is in just over half an hour. I say we do what is necessary." She and Sam strode towards the car park.

Dickie refused a seat and remained standing.

Thabiti asked, "When would you like us to open the bar?"

Dickie considered the question. "I suggest you open with the start of the first match, but don't serve any alcohol until midday. That way we can try to prevent a repeat of yesterday's behaviour."

Thabiti pushed himself up from the table. "Then I'd better restock the fridges with soft drinks." He strolled across the courtyard.

Sergeant Wachira returned waving some sheets of paper which she handed to Dickie and asked, "Are these what you're looking for?"

Taking the sheets, he studied them and beamed. "This is exactly what I need, and it looks as if everything is here."

Sam arrived carrying an array of items, including a horse's boot, a polo stick and a girth, which keeps the saddle on a horse. He held up a small brass ball attached to a rod.

"That's from my bell," exclaimed Dickie. "Did you find all these in Rufus's car?" He shook his head. "This can't continue. But I'm loath to ban Rufus altogether, especially after what Thabiti told us. I need to consider this further." He pursed his lips, turned around and walked back into the clubhouse.

CHAPTER TWENTY-FIVE

R ose sat with Sam and Sergeant Wachira in the courtyard beside the clubhouse. Thabiti appeared carrying a red plastic crate, with the partially worn words 'Coca Cola' printed on it's side.

"I better help Thabiti set up the bar," Sam said as he stood up.

"I need to establish if Rufus Esposito had anything to do with Felix Kamau's death," stated Sergeant Wachira. She turned to Rose and asked, "Do you know where I can find him?"

Rose pushed herself stiffly to her feet. "Let me check when he's playing."

Inside the clubhouse she found the board onto which Dickie had pinned the day's timetable.

"I was just about to carry it outside," said Dickie as he picked the board up. "It's nearly time to start the first match and I'm still not ready."

Sergeant Wachira joined Rose beside the board, which was now propped against the outer wall of the clubhouse. Rose pointed to the timetable and said, "Rufus is playing in the second match, for the Only Fools on Horses. As he's not here, we should find him down at the stables."

"What do you know about the sport of polo?" asked the young sergeant in a conversational tone as they walked unhurriedly across the main polo pitch.

Rose pondered the question. "It brings out the best, and the worst, in people. I enjoy watching the skill of the players and their horses, and the speed of top class polo. It's inclusive in that men and women play side-by-side but, as each player needs several horses, it is an expensive sport.

"Saying that, I've met young polo-mad players who've found jobs in Kenya and moved here purely to play polo, because it's more affordable than the UK or US. That is, unless you're a particularly skilful player and a wealthy sponsor pays you to play on his team."

Sergeant Wachira glanced at Rose and said, "But it's an aggressive sport, and from what I witnessed last night, hostilities clearly continue after the matches have finished."

"Not always," Rose replied. "But the players were fuelled by alcohol and this weekend's tournament is especially important. It is one of the rare occasions in the polo calendar where the players choose their own teams, and they all want to win the prestigious Mugs Mug Cup.

"Usually, the tournament organisers pick the teams so they are evenly matched. So this means that an opponent one week might be next week's team mate. The system works well to keep resentment and tempers in check. But this weekend selectors are also here choosing players to represent Kenya in India next month."

"So there's a lot to play for." Sergeant Wachira glanced across to No. 2 pitch, where some players were cantering their horses in large circles.

"There is. But I doubt any of the players would kill a rival for a place on the national team. Don't get me wrong, they'd all love to be chosen, but polo is a team sport and without the best players beside you, you've no chance of winning. I believe Felix would have been selected, but it's unlikely Rufus will be given his place, not with the way he's played so far this weekend."

The young sergeant rubbed her jaw. "Rufus might not have wanted to kill Felix, just cause an injury which would have put him out of action for a few weeks, or a month."

They approached the stables, which were bustling with activity. Rose grabbed Sergeant Wachira's arm as a syce rode past, leading three polo ponies.

"How does he do that? Surely he needs one hand to control his own horse, so how does he control three ponies with the other?" Sergeant Wachira stared after the syce.

Rose chuckled, "Syces and ponies are well trained. It looked as if his left hand held the reins of the horse he was riding and one other pony, and he's leading the other two with his right hand. He'll also use his legs and body weight to steer and change pace. If he's a good rider, he could bring his horse to a standstill using only the pressure of his bottom."

The young sergeant shook her head and blinked.

A polo player with a scarlet shirt trotted past on a black horse.

Becoming businesslike, Sergeant Wachira asked, "So where will we find Rufus?"

"Let's start near the stable where we found Felix's body," replied Rose.

They walked along the perimeter of the stables until Rose spotted Rufus talking to a group of players who wore a range of coloured polo shirts. They scattered as Rose and Sergeant Wachira approached.

"It's funny how, even without my uniform, people still avoid me," muttered the sergeant. She jogged after Rufus and grasped his arm. When he resisted, she tightened her grip and led him back towards Rose.

They stood at the end of a row of stables, beside a concrete storeroom, whilst preparations for the day's tournament continued around them.

"So Rufus, why were you running away from me?" asked the diminutive sergeant.

Rufus sucked in his cheeks and replied in a defiant tone, "I wasn't. But I need to get ready. I'm playing in the next match." He raised an arm in the air.

"Don't worry, as long as you answer my questions fully and truthfully, we'll soon be finished," assured the young sergeant, as she loosened her grip on Rufus' arm. "I understand you had an argument with Felix Kamau, here, at the stables last night?"

Rufus shook his head. "Did I? Yes, I think I remember now. But who told you that? And why does it matter?"

"We're trying to understand Mr Kamau's movements yesterday evening, and establish exactly how he died."

Rufus squinted, "But I thought someone said Sophia's horse kicked him."

"We haven't confirmed the cause of death but, even so, why was Felix Kamau in Miss Gilbert's stable?"

Rufus gesticulated with his arms. "For any number of reasons. Maybe the horse was distressed, and he tried to calm it? Surely it was just an accident?"

"Perhaps, but did Felix Kamau go into Red's stable whilst you were with him?"

"No," Rufus replied defiantly.

Sergeant Wachira widened her stance and asked, "So what were you arguing about?"

"I can't remember, but I guess it was the same thing we always quarrel about. Felix had everything he wanted, and he could just stroll in and buy horses the rest of us couldn't afford. But the worst thing was, he was so nice. Look how he helped Sophia last week. I think that's what really irked me."

Rose suggested, "If you stop being so hard on yourself, you may find you are kinder to other people and that, in turn, they respond better to you."

Rufus lifted his gaze and puffed up his body, but when he caught Rose's eye, she saw the pain and understanding in them. He sighed and his shoulders slumped.

Sergeant Wachira tapped her foot. "Putting all that aside, you were still the last person seen with Felix Kamau, and you were witnessed arguing with him. His father has important connections and I will soon be pressed to explain exactly how he died, and arrest anyone suspected of being involved. And at the moment, that includes you."

Rufus's eyes opened wide and Rose could almost smell his fear. "But I swear, I wouldn't kill Felix. I might shout a lot, and I'm known for getting drunk and throwing the odd punch. But not murder. I didn't kill him. I'm sure I didn't." His breathing became shallow, and he clenched his fists.

Sergeant Wachira hesitated.

A small voice uttered, "Mama Rose."

Rose looked about until she spotted Chumba's face peering around the side of the storeroom. "What's the matter?" she asked kindly.

Chumba gingerly stepped forward and looked from Rufus to Sergeant Wachira and cringed. Then he ran to Rose's side.

She bent down as he whispered in her ear. "Rufus not hurt Felix. I help Rufus to house on Wild Dog Estate. Felix still alive when we go."

CHAPTER TWENTY-SIX

R ose and Sergeant Wachira returned to the clubhouse and once again sat at one of the picnic tables. The young sergeant's lips were pressed tightly together, and she sat hunched over the table.

Sam brought them both hot drinks and joined them. "I take it you're not making much progress."

Sergeant Wachira gave him a bitter smile.

Rose summarised, "Felix appears to have been a pleasant lad with no clear enemies. He may have had a temper on the pitch, which occasionally bubbled over after a match, but he was considered kind and helpful. Some players may have resented his family's wealth and influence, but is that a reason to harm Felix?"

"And I'm not convinced anyone did try to harm him," muttered Sergeant Wachira. "I've still no idea why he was in Sophia Gilbert's horse's stable. Perhaps we'll never know. The only thing that is certain about last night is the amount of alcohol that was consumed and the haziness of everyone's memories."

The courtyard was filling up with spectators and the first match had started. Three scantily dressed young women, carrying oversized bags, were escorted by a respectable looking gentleman. They sat at one of the few spare tables and looked around attentively.

Sergeant Wachira groaned, sat up and started patting down her shirt and shorts. Commissioner Akida, wearing his casual khaki-green uniform, appeared at the entrance to the courtyard. He spotted them and strode across.

"Habari, everyone," he announced in a cheerful manner. Sam shuffled up, making room for the commissioner to sit down.

"Habari, Commissioner," replied Rose. "You're surprisingly cheerful. I expected you to be annoyed that your Sunday has been disturbed by a suspicious death."

"The death is worrying, but I'm glad to be called away today. My wife invited our overly ambitious coroner, Ms Rotich, to lunch and this is the perfect excuse to avoid it." He looked at Sergeant Wachira and continued, "But you appear troubled by this morning's events."

The sergeant gulped and replied, "To repeat Mama Rose's statement before you arrived. We are looking at the unfortunate death of a young man who was generally well liked, and even-tempered apart from on the polo pitch. Whilst we can't establish why he was in the stable of the horse that kicked and most likely killed him, it is unlikely that there was any malicious intent by another party."

The commissioner tapped the table. "But you know his father is a politician and is already calling for answers. When Ms Rotich finds out, those demands will escalate."

The sergeant's shoulders slumped. "I know. The trouble is, everyone has hazy memories of the party and sequence of events last night. Sam and I were working behind the bar and later in the evening Sam spent most of his time breaking up fights."

The commissioner considered Sam's enormous frame. "Well, you were the right man for the job."

Sam smiled ironically.

"The point is," the young sergeant said, in a frustrated tone, "that we, well I, did not take as much notice as I should of what was happening around me. We don't know when Felix left the party, or if he was with anyone."

"I'm certain he wasn't around at the end, when Dickie Chambers closed the bar and we shepherded everyone out of the clubhouse," Sam confirmed.

The commissioner's expression was grave. "I see what you mean. That makes reconstructing a timeline of events difficult."

"Did you break the news to Felix's parents yourself?" asked Rose.

The commissioner looked across the table at her. "I met them at the Mount Kenya Resort and Spa, before I drove here. His father was angry, and his first thought was that someone wanted to harm him. As you pointed out, Sergeant, he is a powerful man who has become wealthy during his time in office and is bound to have made enemies."

"What about his mother?" Rose pressed.

The commissioner's face softened. "She'd just lost a son. And she looked devastated by the news."

Sam asked, "Are they coming to the polo tournament?"

The commissioner rubbed the back of his neck. "They weren't sure, but once the news has sunk in, I think they will appear. And I suspect," he glanced around the group, "it will be with pomp and ceremony. I fear a man like Kristopher Kamau won't give up the dramatic occasion of his son dying to further his own political career."

The commissioner looked as if the coffee Marina had brought him tasted sour.

The group was silent. Rose heard the sound of a bell and the thunder of hooves on hard ground.

"Can I suggest that I take Commissioner Akida to watch the polo? The second match is a re-run between the Painted Dogs and Only Fools on Horses. It'll be interesting to see how they play after last night, and this morning's events."

Sergeant Wachira pushed herself to her feet. "I'll use the opportunity to talk to the players' syces."

She turned towards the stables but Rose called her back, "You'll be better off heading towards No. 2 pitch. They will be with their charges at the pony lines beside the pitch."

Sam also stood. "Thabiti's unwillingly agreed to run the bar on his own for a short time, so I'll walk with you, Judy. I need to spend some time at the Ol Pejeta Conservancy tent, and it'll give me a chance to study the polo players in action."

CHAPTER TWENTY-SEVEN

As the eight polo players rode onto the pitch, wearing either dark brown or bright yellow shirts, Rose entered the members' tent. Poppy Chambers caught her eye and patted the seat beside her.

As Rose sat down, Poppy whispered, "Where've you been? I was worried you'd miss another exciting match. The first one was so close they had to play an extra 'sudden death' chukka."

As the players lined up in front of the tent, Mr Gilbert ushered Violet inside and sat down beside Rose and Poppy.

As the chatter died down, he whispered, "Phew, we just made it. It's important for Violet to attend church on Sunday mornings as it brings her peace and helps her forget ..."

"Ladies and Gentlemen," boomed Dickie through the microphone.

Rose glanced across at Violet, who did not look calm or peaceful. She was staring at the horses and whimpering.

"The next match," Dickie informed the spectators, "is a rerun of yesterday's thrilling contest between the Painted Dogs, in dark brown, and Only Fools on Horses in yellow."

Dickie fell silent and gulped. He continued in a quieter voice, which was full of anguish, "But it is with great sadness that I have to inform you that Felix Kamau, a member of the Painted Dogs team, died last night as a result of a tragic accident."

Rose raised her eyebrows, but supposed Dickie had to say something. And an accident was better than telling the crowd that the police were investigating his death. That would only spook them.

"As a mark of respect, these two teams are wearing black armbands, and I'd like us all to join them in a minute's silence."

Even the horses stilled their prancing and the only movement was a half-hearted head shake from Red.

After a minute, Dickie announced, in a matter-of-fact tone, "Felix Kamau's place on the Painted Dogs team is filled today by Jasper Armitage."

Mr Gilbert leaned closer to Rose and she noticed his red-rimmed eyes. He asked, "Isn't Jasper riding Sophia's new horse? And why is she on a dark-grey? I'm sure it's not one of hers."

"You're right," agreed Poppy.

"To enable the tournament to continue, the players came to an agreement this morning," Rose explained. "Jasper is borrowing Red, to join the two uninjured ponies he has, and Sophia is riding Felix's new horse, Excalibur, on which Felix gave her a lesson last week."

She looked more closely at Mr Gilbert and asked, "Are you all right? You look exhausted."

He smiled weakly. "It's probably a combination of staying up late last night and sleeping on the sofa in the guest cottage. It'll be a relief when the main house is completed. But it was worth it to attend the party."

Dickie said into the microphone, "I'd like to introduce the match umpire, one of our former top players, Yaro Macharia."

Yaro looked striking as he cantered over to the tent on a gleaming black horse. He sat deep in the saddle, bringing it to a halt, and then stood up in his stirrups. He smiled and raised his umpire stick in acknowledgement before galloping away.

Behind her, Rose heard a woman's clipped voice say, "Yaro looks dashing in his black and white referee's shirt, and he's still one of our best riders. Such a shame he chose to give up polo."

Rose glanced around at the three selectors who were choosing the teams to play in India. One of the smartly dressed African men said, "The accident with the child wasn't his fault. After all, Felix's aggressive challenge brought his horse down, and shattered his confidence."

Play started and Sophia intercepted the ball and struck two consecutive clean shots.

"Isn't that Excalibur? She rides him almost as well as Felix," pronounced the other male selector.

Rose turned to Mr Gilbert and said, "A great start for Sophia."

Mr Gilbert appeared to be in a trance-like state. He shook his head and muttered, "Oh, yes." He turned to comfort his wife, whose hands were clasped around her shaking body as she muttered to herself.

Out on the pitch, the play was frenetic. Rufus shouted, "Good try, Sophia," after the ball she hit rolled past the outer edge of the goalpost.

CHAPTER TWENTY-EIGHT

Thabiti prised open the metal cap of an orange Fanta bottle and asked the young, fair-haired boy, who could barely see over the bar, "Would you like me to pour this into a glass?"

The boy nodded.

Thabiti looked up as Chloe and the timid guest who was staying with her, Dotty, walked into the clubhouse.

Chloe commented, "I see you're on your own. Are Sam and Judy at the Ol Pejeta Conservancy stall?"

Thabiti took the fifty shilling note from the young boy who stretched his arm up to take his glass from the bar. Thabiti handed it down to him and the boy walked slowly across the clubhouse, taking great care not to spill his drink.

Thabiti placed one hand on the bar and beckoned with the other.

Chloe frowned as she drew closer. "What is it?"

Thabiti explained in a quiet voice, "One of the polo players was found dead this morning, in a stable."

Dotty gasped.

Marina entered the clubhouse and joined them at the bar.

Chloe's gaze remained focused on Thabiti as she enquired, in a breathless tone, "An accident?" She looked across at Marina and in a lighter voice asked, "Or is this another case for Mama Rose to investigate?"

Thabiti leaned forward. "I don't think anyone's quite sure. By all accounts, Sam and Judy had their hands full serving at the bar last night. The party was rather lively and Sam spent most of his time breaking up fights and arguments. Mr Chambers had enough and closed the bar early."

"So what?" prompted Chloe.

Thabiti stepped back and from a tray he picked up a pint glass, which he started to polish with a white cloth. "I think Judy's beating herself up because she didn't notice anything amiss, and she didn't prevent the player dying."

Dotty asked, in a shy voice, "Where are the stables?"

Thabiti pointed towards the far wall of the clubhouse. "Across the other side of the main pitch."

"So how could your friend have known what was happening there if she was busy working behind the bar."

Marina turned to her and explained, "I'm sure she couldn't. But she's just been promoted to sergeant and some vindictive fellow officers in Nanyuki would jump at the chance to get her demoted."

"To make matters worse," confided Thabiti, "the victim's father is a prominent and well-connected politician."

Marina winced. "Oh dear, that's not good. I know Chloe joked about Mama Rose, but is she doing anything to help?"

"You know what she's like. She listens and processes information until she joins the dots, which are usually invisible to the rest of us. She was at the stables this morning, when the body was discovered, and she's been hanging around the courtyard this morning. I think she's watching the polo match at the moment. Let's hope she's gathered enough snippets of information to work out what happened."

Thabiti looked up as an African man, whose body bulged in his dark suit, stepped into the bar and looked around the clubhouse.

"And soon," Thabiti finished.

The dark-suited man approached two scantily clad women, who were sitting on a windowsill in the far corner. They batted their eyes and giggled.

"I better get back to the kitchen," announced Marina. "Dotty, can you remind me how to prepare the coronation chicken sauce?"

As Dotty and Marina left, Thabiti asked, "Is Dan here?"

Chloe nodded. "He and Al have gone to watch the polo."

Thabiti wet his lips and asked, "Would you mind helping me? Until Sam returns."

"Of course, this should be fun," Chloe beamed as she joined Thabiti behind the bar.

The shiny-suited man left the clubhouse as Thabiti said, "We're only serving soft drinks until midday." He turned to the two drinks fridges and pointed at one. "I've filled this one with sodas and fruit juices, and restocked the other with beers and some wine."

Thabiti felt the atmosphere change and turned around as Mr Kamau entered the clubhouse. He was followed by his wife, who was speaking earnestly with Commissioner Akida.

Mr Kamau strode up to the bar and looked over Thabiti's shoulder. "Excellent, you have Macallan single malt."

Thabiti opened his mouth, but the words stuck in his throat.

Chloe smiled weakly and said in an apologetic tone, "I'm sorry, but we're not allowed to serve alcohol until midday."

Commissioner Akida broke off his conversation with Mrs Kamau and looked up. "I think we can make an exception for the grieving parents. I'll buy the drinks."

Mr Kamau looked serious, "Thank you, Commissioner, but that's not necessary." He removed his wallet from his back pocket. "But will you join me with a whisky?"

The commissioner's eyes brightened. "How could I refuse?"

"Two double Macallans please," ordered Mr Kamau.

Commissioner Akida turned back to Mrs Kamau and asked, "And what would you like?"

"Is it possible to have a cup of tea?" She replied in a small, quavering voice.

The commissioner raised his eyes at Chloe, who responded, "I'm sure I can organise that."

Chloe stepped out from behind the bar and walked across to the clubhouse entrance.

Mr Kamau replaced his wallet before lifting up both drinks. He passed one to the commissioner and raised his glass. "To my boy, Felix." He knocked back the contents of his glass and slammed it on the top of the bar. "Give me a refill."

He turned to the commissioner, who had only taken a sip of his drink. "Another?"

The commissioner shook his head.

Thabiti hesitated and looked across at the commissioner, who gave him an almost imperceptible nod.

With his glass refilled, Mr Kamau turned back to the commissioner and asked, "So, Commissioner, what progress are you making with your enquires into my son's death?"

Commissioner Akida raised his chin and responded, "I have my best man," he coughed, "uh, woman on the job. As well as some specialist consultants."

A deep female voice boomed, "They wouldn't include a busy-body, grey-haired old lady, would they?"

Thabiti stepped back from the bar and began polishing another glass.

Ms Rotich, Nanyuki's newly appointed coroner, filled the doorway. She stepped into the clubhouse resplendent in a gleaming crimson top, with large puffy sleeves, and matching skirt. Thabiti wondered if she had arrived straight from church.

The commissioner blinked and remarked, "If you are referring to Mama Rose, then I think it's worth mentioning that she's a stalwart member of the polo community, and knows the people involved as well as anyone."

Thabiti shrank back as the commissioner's eyes glanced over him and lit up as he noticed something above his head.

The commissioner turned back to Ms Rotich. In a satisfied tone he revealed, "There's even a portrait of her husband hanging behind the bar."

Mr Kamau stepped closer and stared at Craig's image. "Ah, yes. I remember Craig Hardie." He turned back to his audience. "You see, I was a top class polo player in my day, before the demands of my job, and the needs of the Kenyan people, necessitated that I give it up."

The commissioner eyed Mr Kamau politely but Thabiti was certain he'd spotted him wrinkle his nose.

Mr Kamau continued in a commanding voice, "Craig Hardie walked with a limp but he played polo with tenacity and determination."

He crossed his arms and continued, "Of course, he wasn't a high goal scorer like myself but, to give him his due, he was solid in defence."

Ms Rotich purred, "I'd find it difficult to resist your attack."

She locked eyes with Mr Kamau.

"Excuse me," called Chloe brightly as she attempted to get past Ms Rotich.

"Excellent, tea," exclaimed Ms Rotich, removing the cup and saucer from Chloe's hand. "And do you have any cake or biscuits to go with it? I'm feeling a little peckish and I've had to rearrange my lunch invitation."

The commissioner looked as if he'd been stung by a wasp.

Chloe quipped, "Afternoon tea will be served, as the name suggests, in the afternoon." She turned around and Thabiti thought he heard her mutter something about strength and bulk, but he couldn't catch her exact words.

Ms Rotich sailed across to Mr Kamau and in an oily voice divulged, "As Nanyuki's coroner, and the senior purveyor of justice …"

Commissioner Akida choked on his whisky but Ms Rotich ignored him as she continued, "I'll ensure everything is done to resolve this tragic situation, and as speedily as possible."

She batted her eyelashes and her voice became deep and husky as she murmured, "I'm sure a man in your position doesn't like to be kept waiting, and that you value strength and fullness." The edge of her mouth crept up.

Mr Kamau's eyes roamed over her ample frame, and Thabiti had to fight the urge to flee. He swallowed and picked up another glass, which he polished furiously.

A pleasant, clear voice remarked, "I'm sure you'll fulfil your duty as a public servant, once the police have completed their investigation into my son's death."

Mrs Kamau took the cup and saucer, which Chloe handed her, and said, "Thank you, my dear. I'm sorry to put you to so much trouble." She and Chloe appeared to share a meaningful look.

Chloe moved back behind the bar and muttered, "This is getting interesting."

Mrs Kamau turned to the commissioner and asked, "Tell me about the officer in charge of the investigation."

Commissioner Akida puffed out his chest and replied, "Clearly, I will personally oversee the case, but Sergeant Wachira is the investigating officer. She's one of my best young officers, and she was here last night."

"Good, she sounds like the best woman for the job."

Mrs Kamau glanced at Ms Rotich, who looked as if she was sucking a lemon.

The commissioner nodded.

"Sergeant Wachira is resourceful, perceptive and intelligent."

"And she's probably young and fit and spends her time out in the field, actually searching for answers, rather than trying to impress people with meaningless words."

Mrs Kamau raised her eyebrows.

"Yes, and with your permission I'll go and find out what progress she has made."

The commissioner picked up his cap from the top of the bar, and with a crisp nod in Thabiti's direction, he strode out of the clubhouse.

CHAPTER TWENTY-NINE

Rose was enjoying the quarter-final polo match between the Painted Dogs and Only Fools on Horses, from her seat in the members' tent.

She'd expected the Painted Dogs to run away with it, as they had the previous day, but Only Fools on Horses had changed their tactics and begun to work as a team. For the fourth and final chukka, Sophia once again rode Felix's steel-grey horse, Excalibur.

Poppy remarked, "Now Rufus has stopped shouting at Sophia, and started treating her as a legitimate member of the team, her confidence has increased. And I hadn't realised how solid he was in defence. Oh, that's another shot at goal by Otto that he's knocked back down the pitch."

"And Sophia's reading his game and is straight on the ball. Good try," exclaimed Rose excitedly as Jasper had to gallop across the front of his team's goal, and expertly knock the ball away to prevent Sophia's shot passing between the posts.

Rose turned to Mr Gilbert and said, "Sophia's skill is growing with her confidence. You must be delighted, and very proud. She's young to be playing in this tournament, but she's holding her own."

"Absolutely. Of course," responded Mr Gilbert, but his voice lacked enthusiasm. He tilted his head and looked at Violet with concern. Then he reached into the pocket of his linen jacket and removed a packet of crisps, which he pulled open with a small pop.

He handed the packet to Violet and said, "Here you are my dear, arrowroot crisps, your favourite."

Otto stroked the ball down the pitch and, as Rufus moved to intercept, he neatly passed to Jasper, who scored. Jasper's speed on Red was mesmerising.

Rufus looked disheartened, but he kept his cool and did not shout or rant. Sophia rode across, patted him on the leg and they exchanged words. Both players laughed as play resumed.

"I suspect that's the winning goal," observed Poppy, as Dickie stood and moved towards the table on which his repaired bell stood. "They won't play the extra thirty seconds as the Painted Dogs are now two goals ahead."

Dickie rang the bell, which was followed by a long whistle blast as Yaro Macharia stood up in his stirrups and beckoned to the players to stop. The players shook hands with their opponents, and the captains thanked Yaro.

"That's given us food for thought," said one of the male selectors sitting behind Rose. "I'm delighted Jasper had the chance to play, and he's at the top of his game. Mind you, Rufus's stalwart defence stopped him from scoring several times."

"I was fascinated to see how well Rufus plays when he stops blustering and arguing and actually concentrates on his game," remarked the other male selector.

"There's an interval before the next match. Shall we return to the clubhouse to compare notes and grab a quick drink?" the female selector asked in her clipped voice.

They all stood and strode out of the tent. Mr Gilbert ushered Violet out after them.

Dickie stood before Rose and Poppy with a huge grin. "That was an exciting match, don't you think? Such a shame Only Fools on Horses didn't play like that yesterday, as they could have reached the finals. Still, I hope they're proud of themselves. After all, they're a young team."

Dickie checked his watch. "Time for a quick coffee, ladies, before the next match?"

As Rose walked with Poppy and Dickie along the edge of No. 2 Pitch, her gaze wandered over the delightful surroundings of the Timau polo grounds.

Away to the right, beyond the boundary fence, was open grassland where the landowner's cattle grazed peacefully alongside herds of zebra and impala. She knew elephants occasionally roamed across the polo ground to the coppice of gumtrees which occupied the banks of a stream, and separated the polo grounds from Wild Dog Estate.

Before houses were built on the estate, the woodland had also been a popular residence for a pack of African wild dogs during the summer months.

She heard a shrill, whinnying call which was not made by a horse, but by a bird. She looked up into the azure blue sky at the gliding black kite, with its distinctive forked tail.

The erect figure of Yaro Macharia strode across the main pitch, still wearing the distinctive black-and-white striped umpire's shirt. He carried his helmet and he looked flushed but satisfied.

He joined Rose's group as they reached the top of the bank and cried, "What a fantastic match. The Painted Dogs were always going to win, but it was gratifying to see Only Fools on Horses make them work so hard."

Dickie replied, "You look as if you enjoyed being back in the saddle."

"I did." Yaro laughed. "But don't get any ideas about me returning as a player. I'm getting too old, and having been chained to a desk for several years, my fitness and stamina are not what they used to be."

"Well, I think you cut a fine figure out there," complimented Poppy.

Yaro squared his shoulders and walked into the courtyard with his head held high.

Jasmine Macharia turned round to face the three of them. Her expression was pensive as she observed her husband's flushed face. She bit her lip, and then asked in a girlish voice, "Didn't you miss me?"

"I did, but I had no idea where you were, as you wouldn't answer my calls." Yaro crossed his arms.

Jasmine pursed her lips. "I couldn't. I've lost my phone."

Yaro laughed. "You've lost your phone? How are you coping, not being able to check your social media feeds, or post selfies every few minutes?"

Jasmine's eyes narrowed as she clenched her jaw.

"That was thirsty work. I need a drink," announced Yaro. He turned and strode into the clubhouse.

Rose, Poppy and Dickie helped themselves to tea and coffee. They placed their cups on the edge of a picnic table and surveyed the scene in the courtyard.

The crowd was larger than the previous day and people must have been attracted by the sunny weather, the prospect of a delicious lunch, and the chance to watch some exciting polo.

Rose spotted Chloe's husband, Dan, chatting with the English couple who were staying with them. Marina approached the woman, and they both left, walking towards the kitchen.

Dickie widened his stance and looked about with satisfaction. "It's such a relief that changing the venue has worked. And in many respects it's an improvement on our existing clubhouse."

Rose spotted Commissioner Akida and Sergeant Wachira in deep conversation. It was a pity that the tragic death of a young, talented polo player would always taint the weekend. Rose wondered what progress the young sergeant had made unravelling the previous evening's sequence of events.

The athletic Jasper and fair-haired Otto strode into the courtyard. They both looked dashing in their white breeches, dark brown polo shirts and glowing faces.

The female selector approached Jasper and said, "That was excellent play out there. Continue like that today and you'll be guaranteed a place on the team for India."

Jasper grinned broadly. "Thank you, I'll certainly try."

Yaro appeared beside Rose and remarked, "What a glorious day."

Jasmine glanced towards her husband and a mischievous look crossed her face. She fluffed up her hair and strutted across to Jasper as the selector returned to her group.

Beside her, Rose felt Yaro's body tense. She placed a steadying hand on his arm and he looked around at her with his nostrils flared.

Rose increased the pressure of her grip and explained, "Your wife is an attractive woman, and she knows it. She craves being the centre of attention and having men fight over her."

She looked up at Yaro and asked, "Is that what happened last night? Did she push you too far?"

Yaro bowed his head and replied, "I'm not sure. I can't remember." He glanced across at Rose and then back at his feet. "You don't think I had anything to do with Felix's death, do you?"

Rose watched as Jasmine continued to fawn over Jasper. She heard Jasmine remark in a clear, carrying voice, "You played so well today. And you have such command of that chestnut horse. It made me shiver just watching you."

Jasmine licked her lips and stole a glance at her husband, before leaning towards Jasper and whispering in his ear.

Jasper's face was set, and his eyes darted around the crowded courtyard.

Yaro tensed and attempted to step forward, but Rose held him back. Yaro looked at her with cold eyes.

"Can I suggest a different tactic from barging in and dragging your wife away from Jasper?"

Yaro hesitated.

Rose continued, "Jasper strikes me as a principled man, and whilst he might find your wife attractive, his respect for you prevents him from engaging in her little game. But as long as she continues to illicit jealous reactions from you, she'll continue her flirtatious behaviour."

"What do you suggest I do?" asked Yaro in a deep, stony voice.

"Relax. Approach Jasper and congratulate him on his play today. Even put you arm around him in a brotherly manner, if you feel comfortable."

Rose looked across at Jasmine and Jasper. "Look at Jasper's body language, the way he leans away from Jasmine. And see how his eyes search for someone to rescue him. Let that person be you."

Yaro rubbed his neck. "OK. I'll give it a shot. I wish I'd had your advice yesterday, and I'd been able to read Felix's body language. Perhaps I would have acted less hastily."

Yaro took a deep breath, fixed a smile on his face, and moved towards Jasper and Jasmine. He clapped Jasper on the back and pronounced, "Great play today. I really enjoyed umpiring your match."

Jasper laughed in relief. "And I was grateful to have the chance to play rather than umpire. You should try it, you weren't such a bad player yourself. Weren't you in Craig Hardie's team for his final Mugs Mug? It was my first tournament, and I was certain your team would win."

Yaro's expression was pained as he responded, "And perhaps we would, if our team mate's best pony hadn't been injured."

"Wasn't it brought down?" Jasper asked.

Yaro hesitated, before replying, "It was."

Rose started as she remembered the incident down at Nairobi Polo Club.

Jasper gasped, "Of course, by Felix's father, Kristopher Kamau." He lowered his voice and muttered, "Like father, like son."

"I'm bored with polo talk," announced Jasmine and flounced towards the clubhouse with a calculating expression.

"Kristopher wasn't a bad player, but oh, could he get into a rage if things didn't go his way. Now, I'd better let you prepare for your next match."

Yaro's smile was open and genuine as he called "Good luck," and followed his wife into the clubhouse.

CHAPTER THIRTY

D ickie drained the remainder of his coffee and placed his cup on a picnic table in the courtyard outside the clubhouse. "I must be off, the next match starts shortly."

"And I'd better check on preparations for lunch," remarked Poppy as she left in the direction of the kitchen.

Kristopher Kamau and his wife approached Commissioner Akida. Sergeant Wachira said something to the commissioner and ducked away.

She joined Rose and said, "I'm not ready to face the grieving parents yet. Not until I have some solid answers."

Yaro and Jasmine passed them and stood beside the low wall, between the courtyard and the bank leading to the stables and pitches.

"At least that's one loose end tied up," muttered the young sergeant as she watched Jasmine.

Yaro looked out across the main pitch, but Jasmine turned back to the courtyard and glanced around at the occupants. Her gaze fell on Otto Wakeman, as he flicked his fair curly hair away from his face.

The young sergeant's voice was disapproving as she added, "But it might have been better if she'd stayed out of the way. She behaved dreadfully last night. I've no idea why her husband kept shouting at Felix. It wasn't his fault she was climbing all over him. And now she's eyeing up another victim. Maybe Thabiti's right and she is like a black widow spider devouring her mates."

Jasmine licked her lips.

Rose remarked, "She reminds me more of an alpha female in a pack of wild dogs, as they discard the older males in favour of a younger one, with which they mate."

"Oh, look," murmured the young sergeant, "she's on the prowl."

Jasmine smoothed down her dress and, with her head held high, approached Otto, who was talking with a group of fellow polo players. She draped an arm around his shoulder and whispered in his ear.

Yaro turned around and saw his wife. His face tensed, but as Otto shook off Jasmine's arm and stepped closer to his friends, he smiled in satisfaction. He strode out of the courtyard and down the bank.

Sophia joined her fellow polo players and Otto hugged her. "What a girl. You played beautifully." Sophia blushed.

Jasmine backed away and looked towards her husband, whose distinctive black and white shirt was visible as he mounted a horse which a syce had led across the main polo pitch.

Sergeant Wachira sighed. "Yaro might have learnt how to deal with his wife now, but what damage did she cause last night? Did Yaro tell you how he got his black eye?"

Rose shook her head.

"I didn't see Felix, or anyone else, hit him, despite his increasingly offensive behaviour as he drank more brandy."

Rose gripped her hands in front of her. "He still has no recollection of yesterday evening's events. But I suspect something is nagging at him, and he is worried that he could have been involved in Felix's death."

CHAPTER THIRTY-ONE

Rose joined Poppy in the members' tent beside No. 2 pitch to watch the second chukka of the third quarter-final. It was not as exciting as the previous match between the Painted Dogs and Only Fools on Horses.

When it finished, Poppy announced, "I'm going to help set up lunch. There are more people than we expected, so we've decided to stagger it. And it'll give those playing this afternoon a chance to eat early."

"I'll come with you," said Rose as she stood up.

In the courtyard outside the clubhouse, most of the picnic tables had been pushed together and gazebos erected above them to provide shade for the lunchtime diners, away from the intensity of the sun. It really was a beautiful day and visitors were still arriving.

"Oh dear, the car park's full," observed Poppy. "I do hope there'll be enough lunch for everyone. You know how some people stack their plates with mounds of food, and then leave most of it. I must write a note to stick to the table asking people to take only as much as they can eat."

Poppy left in the direction of the kitchen and Rose sat down at the end of the picnic table, relieved to be back in the shade.

A young, scantily clad African woman and her male companion sat at a table in the sun and observed the new visitors as they entered the courtyard.

Jasper and Sophia walked out of the clubhouse carrying full pint glasses. "I'm still thirsty from our match," remarked Sophia.

"Me too, but these fresh limes and sodas should help," responded Jasper.

They sat down at the table adjacent to Rose, under the shade of the gazebo.

Sophia looked across to where Marina was covering two trestle tables with white table cloths. "I hope lunch is served soon. I'm starving. I never eat before a match."

She looked back at Jasper. "Thank you for stopping me from drinking too much last night. I'd never have played as well today with a hangover. Mind you, it didn't seem to stop Rufus."

Jasper's jaw clenched. "I suppose he's used to it. But just think how good he could be if he stopped getting paralytic at every tournament. And he'd be a far more pleasant individual. He might even start to enjoy life."

"I also wanted to thank you for looking after my dad, and introducing him to people."

"Is he OK this morning? He had a funny turn last night and had to go out for some fresh air. I left before the party broke up, so I didn't see him again."

Sophia smiled indulgently. "He's fine. It's just that he's not used to drinking. We can't keep any alcohol in the house in Nairobi in case Violet finds it."

There was a clatter as Dotty and Marina filled a basket with bundles of knives and forks, wrapped in white paper napkins.

Jasper's eyes narrowed. "Why?"

"Because she literally drowns her sorrows. My dad used to hide his collection of whisky and gins but Violet kept finding it, and on several occasions Dad had to rush her to hospital to have her stomach pumped. It's easier not to keep any drink in the house."

Jasper cleared his throat. "Do you mind me asking why she's like that?"

"Sure, it's not really a secret, but it's very sad." Sophia sipped her drink before continuing, "My mum died when I was little and my dad buried himself in his business. I hardly saw him and was brought up by ayahs. That is, until I found horses."

Sophia smiled. "Anyway, when Violet started working for dad, she was so bubbly and outgoing, and she made him come and watch me at riding competitions, and go to parties and events again in Nairobi. She really brought him out of himself and I was delighted when they got married and had a son."

Sophia paused and sipped her drink again. Dotty and Marina carried stacks of white plates, which they deposited at one end of the trestle tables.

"But they lost Charlie. He was killed in an accident when Violet was pushing him in his pram back from church. You know, the large church just off the Ngong Road, near Jamahuri Park and the Nairobi Polo Club. Anyway, she's never been the same since."

Jasper placed his hand over Sophia's and said, "I'm sorry. That must be so hard for your dad, and for you."

Sophia gulped as she looked into Jasper's concerned eyes.

"Darling," a shrill voice cried. A young, attractive European woman, with long dark hair, flopped onto Jasper's lap and draped an arm around his neck. She wore tailored white shorts which showed off her long tanned legs.

Sophia looked uncomfortable and glanced around the courtyard, which was becoming busier.

"Hi, Olivia," Jasper said in a matter-of-fact tone.

Poppy, Marina, and Dotty carried dishes to the lunch table. Rose could smell the aroma of buttered potatoes.

"Where shall we put these?" asked Marina.

"Can I suggest that if you're worried about people taking too much meat, you put the potatoes, rice, and pasta salad first. We do that at military events so guests fill their plate with the bulky items and have less room for the meats and cheeses." Dotty's cheeks blushed as she placed her bowl on the table.

"Excellent idea," agreed Poppy. "But I'll still pin my notice beside the plates to remind people not to be greedy, although I doubt many will take any notice."

Olivia's loud metallic voice drowned out their discussion. "Jasper darling, I didn't expect to see you here. I thought you'd been whisked over to the UK to play for the Berkshire Mad Hatters.

Don't tell me Selwyn Church has changed his mind." She pouted at Jasper.

A flush spread across Jasper's cheeks.

"Oh," cried Olivia and looked across at Sophia, who was staring across at the lunch table, on which various salads had been placed.

Olivia turned back to Jasper and remarked, "Does your pony fan club not know that you're planning to leave Kenya for a shot at high goal polo?"

"Leave it out, Liv," growled Jasper, as he untangled himself from her embrace. "And we both know Selwyn only recruits top players, especially if they're from minor polo playing countries like Kenya."

Olivia's face was calculating as she responded, "I hear the selectors are choosing the team to tour India." Her eyes narrowed as she looked at Jasper, "If you don't get chosen, will Selwyn withdraw his offer?"

Jasper shifted his weight on the bench and looked down at Olivia's tanned legs.

Olivia peeled herself off Jasper and stood. She looked down at him and remarked in a steely tone, "Well, it's lucky for you that Felix is out of the way."

In the silence that followed, Rose heard Marina declare, "I think we're ready. We've rice, potatoes, bread and pasta salad. Then the other salads and Dotty's coleslaw, followed by the sliced meats, quiches, sausages and the coronation chicken."

Rose turned back to Jasper as Sophia asked in a small voice, "Are you really leaving to play in England?"

Jasper lifted his hands and then let them fall back to the table. "It's a fantastic opportunity, and not one I'm likely to be offered again. But Olivia is right, if I hadn't been able to play today, and if I'm not chosen for the team heading to India, my sponsor will probably change his mind."

Sophia looked down at her hands.

Jasper rolled his shoulders and said, "Cheer up, Soph. Maybe you can join me. Now let's grab some lunch before the hordes descend."

CHAPTER THIRTY-TWO

R ose remained seated at the picnic table, under the shade of a gazebo, in the clubhouse courtyard.

Poppy sat down opposite her, wringing her hands and glancing across at the lengthening queue for lunch.

"Marina and her friends have done an excellent job, but I just hope there's enough to feed everyone. I've kept some back for the officials, selectors and players in the final quarter-final, which should have finished by now."

A beaming Birdie Rawlinson, a fellow member of the East Africa Women's League and one of

Rose and Poppy's friends, approached and said, "Ladies, Terry's going to the bar and asked me to see if you would like a drink."

Rose remembered what Sophia had been drinking and replied, "Can I have a fresh lime and soda?"

"That sounds good," agreed Poppy. "Can I have one of those too?"

Poppy continued to watch the queue for the lunch table, which now snaked around the courtyard to the BBQ area.

A strong, clear voice said, "Sir, I think that's enough. Please come back for more later, but let everyone else get served first."

Poppy beamed and turned to Rose. "Bravo. Who said that?"

A gentleman turned away from the end of the lunch table, revealing Chloe's timid house guest, Dotty, who stood at the far side, monitoring those who were piling food onto their plates.

"Well, well," muttered Rose, "there's more to Chloe's friend than meets the eye."

Birdie returned with their drinks and plopped down next to them. She fanned her flushed face with her hand.

"Was your team playing in the last match?" asked Rose.

"Yes, and it was so exciting. It's Ben's first tournament, and quite a responsibility for him playing with his dad and uncles. But they won by a single goal. They're drawn against the Mane Attraction for their semi-final, whom they should beat. But I think the Painted Dogs will win the tournament, especially now Jasper's back in the team."

Otto Wakeman pushed his grandfather, in his wheelchair, past their table and settled him at a recently vacated table under another gazebo.

Birdie's husband placed her drink on the table before turning to talk to Dickie.

Poppy glanced once more at the lunch queue, which had diminished, and said, "I think we should eat."

CHAPTER THIRTY-THREE

After a delicious lunch, Rose was enjoying a cup of tea in the courtyard beside the clubhouse. Marina and her team were trying to ensure there was enough food left for the remaining guests, officials, and players who hadn't eaten.

"That's the last of the ham," announced Chloe as she placed an oval platter on the lunch table, "so go steady, Thabiti."

Thabiti grabbed another slice of ham whilst Chloe's back was turned and then asked, "Why have you cut the sausages in half? They were small enough already."

Marina shifted from one foot to another and replied in a shrill voice, "Poppy thought they would go further."

Rose grinned. She knew exactly what Poppy had been doing as she hated waste and greedy people.

Poppy had disappeared back to the kitchen after a quick lunch with Rose and Birdie, and Rose was sure she'd scavenged the plates of those guests who'd finished their lunch for anything which could be served again if they were running low on food. This would have included cutting off the ends of partially eaten sausages.

Commissioner Akida sat down next to Rose and remarked, "That's a relief. Kristopher Kamau and his wife have returned to the Mount Kenya Resort and Spa for the afternoon."

He unrolled his knife and folk from their white napkin-wrapping, and added with a grin, "And Ms Rotich left soon after, for which I'm most thankful. Mind you, they all expect answers by the end of today."

Commissioner Akida began to eat as Sergeant Wachira and Thabiti sat down.

Sergeant Wachira asked, "Did you find out anything useful from Felix's parents? Something that could shine a light on his state of mind? And do we know if he was taking drugs, or if he was depressed or had been drinking excessively?"

The commissioner swallowed and replied, "They weren't aware of anything like that, although Felix spent most of his time at his stables, or at one of Kenya's various polo clubs. He told his mother that he felt awful about Jasper Armitage not being able to play in the tournament, and that he was being blamed for it."

Rose thought back to the previous weekend and said, "Because he injured one of Jasper's horses?"

The commissioner's forehead wrinkled. "I don't know anything about that. What he told his mother is that he bought a new horse, in good faith, and wasn't aware that the owner had already agreed to sell it to Jasper. Apparently the owner told him that if he paid a certain amount that day, the horse was his."

Rose sipped her tea and placed her cup on its saucer. "Ah, that'll be Excalibur, which Sophia Gilbert rode so well today. Jasper had agreed to buy him from Brian Ellison so he could play this weekend. He needed another horse as two of his had been injured, and he couldn't ride them."

Sergeant Wachira enquired, "So did Felix take Jasper's place on the team they call the Painted Dogs? I've heard people say they're favourites to win the Mugs Mug Cup."

"That's right," confirmed Rose, "but there was more at stake than just winning this tournament."

Thabiti had been concentrating on his lunch but he now leaned towards Rose and spluttered, "Intrigue. This sounds more like it. Spill the beans."

Rose sat up and flicked a speck of Thabiti's lunch off her sleeve. "Jasper Armitage has been offered a place on a top English polo team. The way it works is that a polo-mad patron, in this case a gentleman called Selwyn Church, pays top class players to be on his team. Selwyn's not a bad player himself, so his team has some success in high goal polo."

Sergeant Wachira tapped her plate with her fork. "So why is that relevant to Felix Kamau's death?"

Rose dropped her voice as a blue-shirted team of players wandered past. "If Jasper isn't chosen to represent Kenya for their tour of India, he could lose his place on the UK team."

"But I watched him play today," said the young sergeant, her eyebrows drawn together, "and he was the best player on the pitch. Particularly on that striking pink horse."

"Strawberry roan," corrected Rose automatically. "But he wasn't guaranteed a place if the selectors couldn't watch him play. In fact, Felix played excellently yesterday and was likely to have been chosen, possibly instead of Jasper."

Thabiti swallowed his mouthful and pronounced, "So Jasper became all friendly with Felix, coerced him into that horse's stable, and made it attack him. All so he can play polo in England. Do you think he'll meet the Queen?"

"Are you creating dramatic solutions for Felix's death?" asked Marina, as she sat down next to Thabiti.

Thabiti pressed a hand to his breastbone and said melodramatically, "I'm offended."

The tension which had built up around the table evaporated as everyone laughed.

Rose composed herself and said in a serious tone, "But Thabiti is right. Jasper is one person Felix would trust and respect, probably enough to persuade him to go into Red's stable. They may have been discussing swapping Red with Excalibur. As we saw today, Excalibur is a far more suitable ride for Sophia Gilbert."

"But surely he wouldn't deliberately make the horse hurt Felix?" queried Marina in an uncertain tone.

"I agree that it seems unlikely," confirmed Rose, "but in the heat of the moment, or if they were having an argument, the horse could have become upset and kicked out. That part I just don't know."

There was silence around the table apart from the sound of Thabiti chomping his lunch.

The commissioner's phone rang and he stood up and walked away before answering it.

"Jasper Armitage does have a strong will and considerable self-control," stated Sergeant Wachira.

"Despite constant jibes from his friends last night, especially that dark-featured Rufus, he only drank a couple of beers. I'm not sure what time he left, but he wasn't there when we had to break up the party."

Rose looked across at the young sergeant and asked, "Have you been able to establish who else was or was not there at the end?"

Sergeant Wachira opened her notebook, flicked through the pages, and consulted her notes. "I don't think our victim, Felix Kamau, was, although I still haven't tied down when he was last seen. Rufus Esposito, we know had an argument with Felix down at the stables, and was taken home by Mama Rose's Chumba.

"Mama Rose, you think you heard them arguing, so that was probably between half nine and ten o'clock. Jasper Armitage, we've already discussed, and nobody saw Mr Macharia after eleven, possibly earlier. His wife, people were less sure about."

Thabiti put down his knife and fork with a clatter and announced, "So any one of them could have been involved."

CHAPTER THIRTY-FOUR

Commissioner Akida returned to the picnic table where Rose was sitting in the courtyard. He straightened his collar and said, "I wish Chloe hadn't told Ms Rotich about afternoon tea. That was her on the phone telling me she's coming back for it, and she's bringing Mr Kamau with her."

He looked at Sergeant Wachira. "She made it clear that I'd better have some answers for her about Felix Kamau's death."

Rose squinted up at the commissioner. "Surely she can't tell you how to run your investigations, can she?"

The commissioner clasped his hands behind his back. "No, but she can make my life difficult, particularly if she has the ear of someone like Kristopher Kamau."

Sergeant Wachira placed her hands on the table and pushed herself wearily to her feet.

"I better get on with the investigation, then. The bars should be open in Timau by now and I need to check Gathi, the syce's, alibi. Felix Kamau sacked him last week, so he has as much reason as anyone for harming him."

Marina stood and began to collect the empty plates.

Sam stepped out of the clubhouse and called, "Thabiti, can you get another crate of Whitecap beers from the ISO container."

The commissioner removed his cap and wiped his brow. "A Whitecap sounds tempting, but I'd better not. It could be a long afternoon."

"Why don't you join me to watch some more polo instead?" suggested Rose. "Most people are down there now, so you never know what snippets of information you might overhear."

Rose and Commissioner Akida sat towards the back of the full members' tent. It was hot and airless and Rose was beginning to feel a little faint. She wished she'd brought a bottle of water with her.

It was the third chukka of the semi-finals and the Painted Dogs were losing by one goal after their opponents, the Saddled and Addled, played an energetic second chukka.

The crowd gasped and Rose looked up. One of the brown-shirted Painted Dogs players had jumped off his horse and was squatting by its front legs.

Dickie jumped up and strode to the front of the tent. He turned around and called, "Rose, I think you're needed."

She gave the commissioner an apologetic smile and rushed after Dickie onto the pitch. A syce ran past her, leading a bay horse.

He handed the reins to the dismounted player, who expertly jumped up and swung his leg over the back of the saddle and sat up on the horse. It was Otto Wakeman.

Otto looked down at Rose and Dickie and said, "I suspect he's pulled a tendon," he indicated with his polo stick towards the horse, which the syce now held. Its head was bowed and sweat glistened on its neck. "I just hope it's not too serious."

"Can he walk?" asked Dickie, as he rubbed the back of his neck.

The syce tugged the reins and the horse almost hopped a stride as he tried not to put any weight on his injured front leg.

"Keep going," instructed Dickie. "Back towards the stables. We have to clear him from the pitch before we resume play."

He watched the horse's slow progress before turning to Rose and asking, "Can I leave you to tend to him? I need to restart the match, or we'll run out of time to play the final."

Dickie returned to the members' tent as Rose followed the injured horse towards the stables.

CHAPTER THIRTY-FIVE

As Rose approached the Timau Polo Grounds stables, she heard raised voices and, when she turned a corner she was confronted by Gathi shaking a finger in Chumba's stricken face.

Gathi taunted, "See what happens when you steal someone's job? My job. And now you'll also lose yours. Bwana Felix is dead and guess who the police will blame?"

He jabbed Chumba in the chest. "The person who found his body. That's you. So you'll be locked up in prison."

Rose strode forward and grabbed Gathi's arm. "That's enough, you bully. He's a child, and he was only helping Felix because you didn't do your job properly."

Chumba said in a timid voice, "Mama Rose, they won't lock me away, will they?" he sniffed. "I liked Bwana Felix. He good to me."

Rose glared at Gathi, who shrank back and then slipped away. She turned to Chumba and replied, in a gentle voice, "No, they won't lock you away. Now, I need your help."

Chumba wiped his eyes and looked up expectantly. "Can you fetch my veterinary bag? My car is parked near the clubhouse with the other cars." She fished her keys out of her trouser pocket. "Here's the key."

Chumba smiled and dashed off.

Rose looked around for her patient. He was standing outside a stable with his injured leg bent and the point of his hoof touching the ground.

She walked across and bent down to remove the neoprene boots, which were wrapped around both front legs to protect them from knocks and other wounds. The injury was obvious. The back of the leg nearest to her was bowed out below the knee.

She ran her hand down the horse's leg and it felt warm and squidgy. Her priority was to cool it and reduce the swelling.

"Can you fetch a bucket of cold water and a sponge," she instructed the syce. "I'll hold your horse."

Ruptures and tears in the long leg tendons were common injuries amongst sports horses, especially those which gallop, jump, or turn quickly on hard ground.

To prevent long-term damage, the amount of blood and inflammation needed to be reduced, which is done by cooling the area.

The syce returned with a full bucket of water and Rose bent down and picked up the partially submerged sponge. She explained, "You need to fill this sponge with water."

She demonstrated by placing the sponge back in the bucket, "And squeeze it so water runs down the back of the leg. Just placing the full sponge against the leg won't have the same effect."

Gathi wandered towards them and leaned against the wooden entrance rails of a stable as he watched them work. He was chewing a piece of straw, the end of which protruded from his mouth.

Rose ignored him and handed the sponge to the syce. "You have a go." Gingerly, he did as she instructed.

She thought she heard a boda boda.

Chumba appeared, bent under the weight of her green veterinary bag, which he carried on his back. He deposited it on the ground and rocked on his unsteady legs. Rose found her syringes and needles and injected the horse with an anti-inflammatory drug.

She turned as Sergeant Wachira marched towards her.

The young sergeant's face was set as she stared over Rose's shoulder and called, "You're a lucky man, Gathi. It took me a dozen attempts to find the bar you were drinking in last night, in Timau. But the bartender remembered you clearly. You got into a scuffle with one of his regulars and he had to throw you out."

Gathi continued to lean nonchalantly against the wooden rails.

Sergeant Wachira stopped and stood with her legs planted wide apart. "But I am confused about your movements after that. The bartender thinks it was around half-past nine when you left, but you told us about Rufus and Felix's argument, which was around the same time. None of the boda boda drivers remember bringing you back here, so when and how did you get back?"

Gathi spat out the piece of straw he was chewing. "You police are all the same. Always so quick to blame us syces. What about your posh friends up at the clubhouse? I bet you're not questioning them and accusing them of killing Felix."

The young sergeant crossed her arms and her voice was louder as she explained, "I'm not accusing you, or anyone else, of killing Felix Kamau. I'm merely trying to do my job and establish when and how he died."

Gathi stood up and looked around. Nearby, a group of syces laughed.

"I'm still waiting," said Sergeant Wachira as she tapped her foot on the ground. "How and when did you get back to the stables?"

Gathi shuffled his feet. "OK. If you must know, I didn't return until this morning. I fell asleep in a shop doorway, but it was cold and I woke up shivering. I walked back and as I arrived, I overheard two syces discussing the row Felix and Rufus had last night."

"But you didn't witness it?"

"No." Gathi stared at the ground.

Rose wondered who she had seen in the shadows the previous evening.

One of the syces in the nearby group finished eating some crisps. He blew into the empty packet and then clapped his hands together. There was a loud bang.

Chumba jumped and yelped. He hid his face in his hands.

"Chumba, what's wrong?" asked Rose.

"That's the noise I heard last night."

"When?" pressed Rose.

Sergeant Wachira drew nearer.

Beside them, Otto Wakeman's syce continued to bathe Otto's horse's injured leg.

"When I came back from helping Rufus home. It was dark, and the noise made me jump. I fall over." He looked up with wide, stricken eyes.

Rose held eye contact with Chumba. "Did you see or hear anyone?"

"I heard the horses. The noise upset them and they whinnied, snorted, and some of them kicked at their stables. But I didn't see anyone." He looked down at his feet and whispered. "I am really scared so I just lie on the ground."

"What did you do when you did get up?" Sergeant Wachira asked.

"I checked Bwana Felix's horses. One had knocked over its water bucket, so I refilled it. Red was still snorting, but he calmed down when I went across and stroked him."

Chumba gasped, "Do you think Bwana Felix was lying in his stable. Is it my fault he's dead?"

Rose placed her hand on the boy's shoulder. "No, Chumba, it's not your fault Felix is dead."

CHAPTER THIRTY-SIX

Rose had walked back to the clubhouse with Sergeant Wachira, but when she saw the crush of people inside, she settled herself at a picnic table in the courtyard, under the shade of a gazebo.

She was still mulling over Gathi's admission. She was certain someone had been hiding in the shadows at the stables when she and Poppy walked past on Saturday evening.

But if Gathi had been in Timau, it must have been someone else. She wondered who.

Poppy, Marina and Chloe appeared. Poppy looked at her watch and checked, "You're sure you'll be ready in ten minutes."

Marina nodded, "We're only waiting for hot water. But it's a good job we found that electric kettle or we wouldn't have had any."

Poppy joined Rose as Chloe entered the clubhouse, and Marina turned back towards the kitchen.

"Trouble?" asked Rose.

"We ran out of gas. I thought we could use the smaller gas bottle, but that's almost empty from frying eggs for breakfast. Luckily Marina found an electric kettle, but it means afternoon tea is delayed."

"Is that why it's so full in the clubhouse?"

"I guess so. But at least we get a few minutes' peace out here." Poppy removed her glasses, allowing them to hang around her neck on their beaded chain. She wiped perspiration from her forehead.

"Maybe not," said Rose in resigned tone as three large black Land Cruisers, with tinted windows, drew up and stopped by the entrance to the courtyard.

Two tough-looking young men got out and looked around. One turned back to the middle car and opened the door.

A beaming Ms Rotich climbed out, followed by Kristopher Kamau. Ms Rotich smoothed down her garish yellow and green dress and followed Mr Kamau into the clubhouse.

As the wheels of the black cars skidded in the sandy ground, and the cars sped away, Poppy asked, "How was Otto's polo pony?"

"The tendon is badly bowed. We'll have to see what it's like once we get the swelling down, but Otto won't be able to play him again this season," replied Rose.

"Oh dear, that's two ponies down for the Painted Dogs."

Rose's eyes widened. "You mean they won their semi-final. They were a goal down when I left."

Poppy leaned back and said in an appreciative tone, "Jasper was like a one-man whirlwind. He and Red performed two solo runs from just in front of their own goal posts, all the way up the pitch to score. In the end, the Painted Dogs won by two goals."

Commissioner Akida stepped into the courtyard from the direction of the polo pitches, nodded towards Rose and Poppy, and followed Ms Rotich into the clubhouse.

CHAPTER THIRTY-SEVEN

Thabiti's stomach churned as more people entered the already packed clubhouse.

He wished Judy wasn't still investigating Felix Kamau's death. Even so, he'd consider changing places with her rather than face the crush of people in front of the bar. At least Sam had returned from the Ol Pejeta Conservancy tent to help.

"Oi, I asked for two Tuskers," an impatient voice shouted.

Thabiti turned and removed two bottles of beer from the fridge. In a mechanical motion, he removed their caps and handed them to a red-faced man.

The man slapped a five-hundred shilling note on top of the bar.

Chloe pushed her way through the growing crowd and pronounced, "Marina sends her apologies. We ran out of gas so the large kettles haven't boiled. We've found a small electric one in a storeroom, but afternoon tea will be delayed by ten minutes."

"Barman," a woman shouted.

"Can you help us?" Thabiti pleaded. He took a deep breath, turned towards the woman, and asked, "What would you like?"

"Some service," a younger man called.

Chloe smiled and replied, "Of course, what can I get you?"

The level of noise in the room dropped, and the crowd parted as Kristopher Kamau strode effortlessly towards the bar. The enormous figure of Ms Rotich followed in his wake.

A scantily clad woman brushed past Mr Kamau. She stopped and gave him an apologetic smile as she mouthed, "Sorry."

Sam growled beside Thabiti.

Thabiti looked from Sam to Mr Kamau and frowned. He had the feeling he was missing something.

Sam beckoned to Commissioner Akida, who had appeared in the clubhouse entrance.

Chloe smiled brightly at Kristopher Kamau and asked, "What would you like?"

"A double whisky, Macallan, if you still have some. None of that blended rubbish." He turned to Ms Rotich. "Will you have the same, Fatima?"

"Of course," the coroner drooled.

Chloe poured the drinks and placed them on the bar. "That's two thousand shillings."

Mr Kamau reached into his back trouser pocket and froze. "Where's my wallet?"

Ms Rotich's eyebrows drew together as she asked, "Did you leave it in the car?"

"No, I definitely had it."

Sam leaned forward. "These drinks are on the house." Then he whispered something to the commissioner, who turned and pushed through the crowd, back towards the entrance door.

Kristopher Kamau indicated to one of his security men.

Judy, who appeared to still be in her sergeant's role, was speaking to a group of blue-shirted polo players. She turned and exchanged words with the commissioner.

Thabiti realised a customer was speaking to him. He leaned forward and said, "Sorry, what was that?"

As he handed the man a Whitecap beer, Sam whispered in his ear. "Don't make this obvious. Pretend you're collecting glasses or something, but go and stand by the fire escape door. And don't let anyone out."

Thabiti narrowed his eyes at Sam.

Sam handed him a round, black tray and whispered, "Go."

Thabiti pushed his way between groups of people who were either chatting loudly or drinking thirstily.

At the closed fire escape door, he turned and observed Sam nod to Commissioner Akida. Chloe looked flustered as she managed the bar on her own and people shouted at her from various directions.

Judy climbed onto a chair, pushed against the side wall, and Thabiti watched as Sam pointed towards the centre of the room.

Thabiti stiffened and felt his eyes bulge as Judy appeared to dive off the chair into the throng. The crowd parted in front of her as she leapt three paces and grabbed hold of a young, scantily dressed woman.

"Hey, let go of me," cried the woman.

Judy peered into the large bag the woman carried over her shoulder. She looked up, and with raised eyebrows, declared, "Not a chance. You're coming with me."

Thabiti caught a darting movement out of the corner of his eye, and a hand push him forcefully in the back. He dropped his tray but managed to spin around and seize the arm of another scantily dressed woman as she was about to push open the fire escape door.

"Get off me," the woman cried.

"Why? Where are you going?" His hands felt moist as he struggled to keep hold of the squirming woman.

People stopped their conversations and stared at Thabiti. He felt his ears redden.

The fair-haired Otto Wakeman pushed through a group of onlookers and said, "Here, let me help."

Thabiti adjusted his grip and as he and Otto finally restrained the woman, he heard Sophia Gilbert ask, "Aren't those girls with you?"

There was a scuffle near the fireplace and a man cried out in pain. Sam dived into the melee and there was the sound of clapping as he reappeared, leading a third young woman and a smartly dressed, red-faced man towards the entrance door.

"I'll take this one to join her friends." Otto dragged the young woman away as she continued to resist and twist around in his grip.

The volume of conversation increased dramatically as Thabiti picked up his tray and rejoined Chloe behind the bar.

"What was all that about?" exclaimed Chloe.

Thabiti shrugged his shoulders. "I've no idea."

CHAPTER THIRTY-EIGHT

arina and Dotty placed trays of sandwiches on the lunch tables, which were now pushed back against the clubhouse wall.

Rose and Poppy were silent for several minutes until Rose heard clapping and turned to Poppy. "Was Dickie making an announcement?"

"He can't be. He hasn't come up from the pitch yet."

Sergeant Wachira marched a young woman out of the clubhouse. Sam, who gripped the arms of another young woman and an angry-looking man soon followed her.

Rose remembered seeing them in the morning. Both women carried large cotton bags which appeared fuller, and heavier, than when they'd arrived.

"Will you get off me," screamed a third woman as Otto Wakeman escorted her out of the clubhouse.

"I've no idea what you've done. But you're not getting away with it," Otto declared.

"Thank you, young man," commended Commissioner Akida, as he took the arm of the struggling woman.

Otto strode back towards the entrance of the clubhouse but stopped to allow Jasmine Macharia lead her husband out.

His head was bowed and there was blood on the front of his black and white umpire's shirt. He held a tissue to his nose, which was also stained red.

Poppy stood up and called, "Jasmine, over here. What happened?"

"Yaro tried to restrain that man," Jasmine indicated towards the smartly dressed man who

Sam was still holding, "and he swung round and hit Yaro on the nose."

Yaro sat on the bench, facing away from the picnic table. Rose stood in front of him and suggested, "Tip your head back rather than forward, and if it's not too sore, pinch it just above the bridge. That should help reduce the bleeding."

Yaro bent his head back but still held the tissues to it. With his free hand, he touched his nose but cried, "Ow."

A loud clatter caused them to look up as an array of items cascaded onto a picnic table. Sergeant Wachira grunted as she held one of the young women's bags upside down.

Commissioner Akida inhaled and announced, "That's quite a collection." He sifted through the items. "Mobile phones, wallets, jewellery."

Sergeant Wachira tipped another bag onto the table and Rose gasped. The gold tankard which she had given the polo club, to be presented in Craig's memory, fell out. It was the second time someone had stolen it.

Last month the young sergeant had discovered it in the coroner's office after Ms Rotich had unknowingly bought it from thieves who had burgled Rose's cottage.

Dickie strode over and announced, "What a relief. I've been looking for that trophy everywhere."

Sam said, in a quiet voice, "I suggest we search for Kristopher Kamau's wallet and return it to him quickly."

"Agreed," replied the commissioner. He stopped and tilted his head to one side. "And I hear a car. Hopefully, it's the Timau police arriving to collect our suspects."

An old-style, long-wheelbase Land Cruiser ground to a halt by the entrance to the courtyard. Two policemen jumped out and hastily placed their white caps on their heads. They ran towards the commissioner and saluted.

"Very good," nodded the commissioner. "Here are your prisoners. Please secure them in your vehicle and then one of you can take them back to the police station. I want the other one to photograph and log all these items."

"Can't we do that at the station?" a policeman asked.

"No, we need to itemise every item and return them to their owners. Start by finding Kristopher Kamau's wallet."

The policeman who had spoken gulped, "You mean the politician?"

"That's exactly who I mean," replied the commissioner.

CHAPTER THIRTY-NINE

Marina walked across the courtyard carrying two thermos flasks, and Dotty followed with a large cafetière. They placed them on the tables beside the platters of sandwiches and cake stands piled with cakes and biscuits.

Poppy Chambers strode across and asked, "Are we ready?"

"Yes," replied Marina. Her face was flushed.

Poppy joined her husband, who was still staring at the array of stolen items piled on a picnic table. "Please, can you let everyone know that afternoon tea is ready."

Dickie turned, but the commissioner placed a restraining hand on his shoulder. "Just a minute. We'd better put these away first. We don't want everyone grabbing their possessions before we've had a chance to document them."

Rose turned her attention to Yaro Macharia, who was still sitting with his head tilted back. "Let's see if the bleeding has eased."

She lifted Yaro's hand, and the tissue he was clutching, away from his nose. "Just a trickle,' she said with satisfaction.

"Do you mind if I get a cup of tea?" Jasmine asked in a quiet voice. She looked at her husband with concern. "Would you like anything?"

"No, thank you."

As Jasmine walked away, Yaro whispered, "I've remembered."

Rose drew her eyebrows together. "Remembered what?"

"What happened last night."

"Go on," said Rose slowly.

"Jasmine was behaving appallingly and was all over Felix. I should have felt sorry for him, but the drink made me so jealous and angry. After supper, she disappeared and Otto told me he thought he'd seen her walking towards the stables, so I followed you and Poppy down there.

"I heard arguing and went to investigate, but it wasn't Jasmine. It was Rufus, and he was really drunk. Felix remained calm but Rufus was shouting and cursing him until he fell over. Felix left Rufus and walked away but I spotted a young syce help Rufus out of the stable area."

"Were you hiding in the shadows?" asked Rose.

Yaro pressed his lips together and tried to lower his head, but Rose placed a hand under his chin to keep it tipped back.

Yaro continued, somewhat awkwardly, "I think so. I couldn't find Felix or Jasmine, and I stumbled up and down the rows of stables. Eventually I heard Jasmine laugh, and I found her astride Felix, who was sitting on a bale of hay, with his back pressed against a stable. He was holding Jasmine's arms, and I thought they were being intimate, but now I think he was trying to fend her off.

"Of course, I was furious and charged straight in without thinking. Jasmine jumped up and do you know, she had a look of triumph on her face. Of course, I didn't register that at the time, but I hurled myself at Felix, who was on his feet by then. He neatly side-stepped me and I carried straight on and banged my head against a wooden rail."

He winced. "No wonder my nose is so sore. That's the second time it's been hit."

Jasmine returned and held a plate of cakes and sandwiches towards her husband. He reached up with his hand and Rose saw he was struggling to take one.

"OK, I think you can sit up now."

Yaro reached for a scone, smothered in jam and cream. He took a bite and then mused, "But I've no idea how I got this black eye."

Jasmine sat meekly at the table and sipped her tea.

"I suspect it's a result of hitting your nose," stated Rose. "Fluid from your injured nose may have filled the loose cavities around your eyes and broken some of the smaller blood vessels, causing the bruising around your eye."

"You're such a hero," purred Jasmine. "Everyone's talking about you, and how you confronted that man." She leaned closer and whispered, "Apparently, he and his companions have been stealing from the guests and players all weekend, but nobody noticed. I bet they're the ones who took my phone."

Rose turned to Jasmine. "What did you do last night after your husband tried to attack Felix?"

She placed her hand on her chest and replied, "He thought he was defending my honour. How sweet. I helped him back to the clubhouse, but he wasn't really with it, so I put him in his car to sleep."

"And what about you?"

"Oh, I returned to the clubhouse, but it was rather boring. A friend mentioned a nightclub in Timau, so a group of us left and went there. I'm not sure what time we eventually arrived back at my friend's house."

"And you left your husband here?"

Jasmine looked at Rose with an innocent expression. "Well, I couldn't take him with me."

CHAPTER FORTY

P oppy Chambers placed two cups of tea and a plate of sandwiches on the picnic table. Rose picked up an egg and cress sandwich and watched the groups of players and spectators in the clubhouse courtyard.

Jasmine Macharia sat beside her husband, and fed him cakes.

Dickie shook hands with Commissioner Akida and strode over to join them.

"Tea, dear?" asked Poppy.

"Is there coffee? I need to keep my wits for the final, and any other unexpected events." He lowered his voice. "I can't believe none of us noticed that gang hanging about and stealing from us."

Poppy walked across to the tea table.

"There were so many new people here this weekend, and they mingled with the crowd. So how did you find out?" asked Rose.

"Sam, our sharp-eyed temporary barman."

Rose picked up her cup of tea. "He'd been muttering about undercurrents and something being amiss. It must be from his training and undercover work in Kenya's Anti-poaching Unit."

Poppy returned and handed Dickie a cup.

"Thank you." He turned back to Rose and enquired, "But I thought he worked for Ol Pejeta Conservancy."

Rose sipped her tea and placed her cup back on its saucer. "He only recently became their Director of Operations. Before that he was a Kenya Wildlife Officer and spent the last few years infiltrating and breaking up poaching gangs."

Dickie finished a ham and salad sandwich and replied, "Well, I'm thankful for his vigilance. It would have been a disaster for the polo club, and the Timau Polo Grounds, if the thieves had got away. The police located their car and found more stolen items in it, presumably from yesterday.

At least we can hand everything back to the rightful owners after prize-giving. I'm grateful to the commissioner for recording all the items here rather than taking them back to the station. It'll prevent a lot of unpleasantness"

Rufus Esposito and Sophia Gilbert poured themselves glasses of water from the tea table.

Sophia commented, "I can't believe you're drinking water, Rufus."

He smiled serenely and replied, "I could murder a beer, but I'm going to wait until after the prize-giving."

They joined Otto and other players beside a nearby table.

Dickie Chambers turned to Yaro and asked, "Are you all right to umpire the final?"

Jasmine plumped herself up and exclaimed, "Can't you see he's injured? He's been so brave," she cooed. "And he does look dashing in his umpire's uniform, astride his horse. But now he needs to rest." She licked her lips and placed her hand on Yaro's thigh.

Yaro gulped and gazed intently at his wife.

Dickie rolled his eyes. "I'd better find another umpire then." He looked around.

Rufus turned around and asked, "Are you looking for an umpire?"

Dickie hesitated.

Rufus held up his glass of water and grinned. "I promise, I haven't been drinking."

"Give him a chance," prompted Rose. She lowered her voice and added, "He needs someone to believe in him."

"OK, but I'd feel happier if you had someone to help you. This will be a fast-paced match," declared Dickie.

Rufus tugged Sophia's arm.

"What?" she remarked as she turned around.

"Do you fancy umpiring this last match?" asked Rufus.

A flush spread up her neck and into her cheeks. "Me? I don't know how to umpire. And certainly not the final."

"Not by yourself," Rufus laughed. "But will you help me?" He lowered his voice but Rose heard him whisper, "Mr Chambers doesn't trust me on my own." He grinned at Sophia.

Sophia hesitated. "OK, but which horses shall I ride? I was just discussing with Otto and Jasper which extra polo ponies they need for the final."

"What about Excalibur?" asked Otto.

Jasper shook his head. "Not with Kristopher Kamau watching. Just imagine if he was injured, or worse. But I think Sophia will be fine umpiring on him."

"You can ride Dillion and Jemima," offered Rufus as he maintained eye contact with Jasper.

"But they're your best polo ponies. My recent record with horses isn't great and the Hot to Trots are all fired up to beat us. It'll be an aggressive match."

Rufus shrugged. "I know. But they're great ponies and although they're both past their best, they deserve to be in the winning team. They probably would have been if I'd taken polo a little more seriously."

Jasper slapped Rufus on the shoulder. "Thanks, mate."

Rufus beamed.

Jasper turned to Sophia and asked, "Are you nervous?"

She nodded.

"The main thing is safety, and after that it's keeping the game flowing. Now that's not always easy if players are coming on and off each other's lines, so if you're not sure, defer to Rufus. He's had plenty of practice at holding his own."

Jasper put his arms around Rufus and Sophia, and declared, "Let's do it."

They all strode off towards the stables.

CHAPTER FORTY-ONE

The members' tent beside No. 2 pitch was full when Poppy and Rose arrived. Poppy had insisted on chatting to Marina in the kitchen.

"There's no point letting all that food go to waste," she told Rose. "We might as well serve the leftover cakes and sandwiches to those who stay for the prize-giving."

They entered the tent and looked around. Dickie indicated to two chairs, on the second row, on which he'd placed his clipboard and hat. He'd pinned a notice with "Official" to the chair on the end of the row, which Rose presumed was for himself.

As they sat down, Poppy glanced towards the far end of the front row and whispered, "I'm pleased we're not sitting behind the coroner. We wouldn't see a thing."

Ms Rotich had squeezed her large frame onto a white plastic chair which was buckling under her weight.

She seemed totally unaware as she turned to Kristopher Kamau and announced, "So, each team has four players. But they change horses every few minutes. Is that really necessary?"

Rose spotted Birdie and Terry Rawlinson sitting further along her row, ready to watch their sons and grandson play in the final for the Hot to Trots. She leaned forward and whispered, "Good luck."

"Oh, thank you, Rose," replied Birdie. "I think they'll need it, but it's so exciting being in the final."

The selectors arrived and sat in front of Rose and Poppy, in seats Rose presumed Dickie had reserved for them. She turned and looked towards the back of the tent. Mr Gilbert, Sophia's father, looked very pale. He popped something into his mouth and drank from a bottle of water.

Violet's head was bowed as she stared down at her hands, which were constantly moving in agitation. Her husband offered her a packet of crisps, which she munched noisily.

Commissioner Akida, Sam, Sergeant Wachira and Thabiti strode past the front of the tent. Sam stopped and exchanged words with Dickie that Rose couldn't catch.

Thabiti entered the tent, stood at the end of their row and whispered loudly, "We've closed the bar for the final. I'm actually quite excited about it. We're watching the match from the Ol Pejeta Conservancy tent."

The players rode onto the pitch and for the final time lined up in front of the members' tent.

"Magnificent," cried Ms Rotich.

Dickie cleared his throat and said into the microphone. "Ladies and Gentlemen. Welcome to the 2016 Final of the Mugs Mug Cup. In brown, we have the Painted Dogs and in red, Hot to Trot."

As Dickie introduced the team members, Rose admired their gleaming ponies. They pawed the ground, shook their bridled heads and chomped on the metal bits in their mouths. The players all wore serious, determined expressions.

Dickie finished his introductions and Rose joined the rest of the spectators as they clapped in appreciation.

The players rode away and Dickie called, "Umpires please."

Rufus sat squarely on his bay horse and beamed at the spectators.

Sophia's face was flushed and she looked nervous as she patted Excalibur's dark-grey neck.

Rose heard Mr Gilbert say, "Jasper was right last night. Excalibur is more suitable for Sophia at the moment than Red."

Dickie said into his microphone, "I'd like to thank all the umpires this weekend. Without them, the tournament could not take place. Jasper Armitage for all his hard work yesterday. Yaro Macharia for getting back on a horse today, and I hope we'll see more of his excellent riding skills in the future. And for the final, two of our younger players are officiating. Rufus Esposito and Sophia Gilbert. Good luck to you both."

Rufus held up his umpire's stick as he saluted the crowd before turning his horse on its haunches and cantering away. The teams lined up in front of him and play began.

Sophia and Rufus must have found clean umpire shirts to wear, as neither one was covered in Yaro Macharia's blood. Rose hadn't seen Yaro or Jasmine in the members' tent. Her thoughts drifted away from the polo.

Had Yaro and Jasmine been the last people to see Felix alive? Or had someone else joined him down at the stables?

It seemed unlikely that Yaro had been involved in Felix's death, as every account of him was that he'd been very drunk. And Thabiti said Yaro had been in a state when he'd woken up in his car this morning.

But what about Jasmine? Had Felix rejected her and had she returned to take her revenge? Perhaps she'd come back to finish what she'd started? Rose shook her head. That was unlikely, as Jasmine liked an audience and to have her husband rescue or fight over her, and he'd been asleep in his car.

The crowd clapped and cheered. Hot to Trot had scored the first goal.

CHAPTER FORTY-TWO

The first chukka of the Mugs Mug final finished with the Hot to Trot team ahead by two goals to one. Rose leaned forward and congratulated Birdie Rawlinson. "Great teamwork."

"Wasn't it just? And young Ben scoring a goal, he'll be so chuffed."

Rose sat back and Poppy whispered, "I don't think we've seen the best play from the Painted Dogs."

Neither did Rose. She suspected the players had ridden their slower horses as they'd struggled to keep up with the Hot to Trot team.

Jasper Armitage cantered onto the pitch astride Sophia Gilbert's horse, Red.

"Now we should get some pace," remarked Poppy, and Jasper immediately sped after the ball as play resumed. The crowd gasped as he scored one, and then a second goal in quick succession, putting the Painted Dogs in front.

Jasper was electric, and he and Red moved like a blur across the pitch.

Just how much did a place on a high goal polo team in the UK mean to Jasper? And would he have killed Felix to keep it?

Rose tapped her legs. Felix alive did not preclude Jasper from being selected for the Kenyan team touring India. Equally, Felix dead did not guarantee his selection, although as she watched him speed up the pitch and score another goal, she didn't see how the selectors could possibly leave him out.

It was only because of Felix's death that Jasper had the opportunity to play today and show everyone that he was a top class polo player.

Jasper said he left the party early, but did he go straight home? Or did he visit the stables? And why would Jasper want to harm Felix in the middle of the tournament rather than before it started?

Perhaps he hadn't expected Felix to play so well, and felt his position on the Kenyan team was under threat. Maybe it was revenge for Felix purchasing a horse he'd already agreed to buy, which meant he couldn't play in the tournament, and which jeopardised his whole future.

Some of the spectators rose to their feet and applauded as Dickie rang the bell to signal the end of the second chukka.

Poppy continued her analysis of the game. "The Painted Dogs are two goals ahead, but I think they've played their ace with Jasper and Red. Now they'll have to work hard to maintain their lead. Jasper's riding Biscuit for the third chukka. He's dependable and willing to get involved, but he's not as quick as Red."

Play resumed.

Chumba had told her the horses had been agitated last night, and he'd had to calm Red.

But was that before or after Felix had entered Red's stable?

It was very likely that the shouts and arguments, firstly between Rufus Esposito and Felix, and then Yaro and Felix, had upset the horses.

Maybe Felix had the same idea as Chumba, but whilst Chumba had stayed outside Red's stable to placate the horse, perhaps Felix had gone inside.

Then there was the loud popping noise which had scared Chumba, and presumably the horses. What had made that? Had someone fired a gun?

Was Kristopher Kamau right and someone had wanted to take revenge on him by harming his son? Felix could have hidden from attackers in Red's stable and when a warning shot was fired, the frightened Red had kicked out.

But none of the syces had mentioned strangers or gun shots. She thought it likely that Gathi would have revelled in telling her or Sergeant Wachira something like that. Knowing Gathi, he would probably have demanded a reward for such important information.

The third chukka was relatively uneventful. The Hot to Trot team scored a penalty shot and Otto just managed to caress the ball over the line to keep the Painted Dogs in front.

Dickie rang the bell for the end of the chukka.

"This is it," announced Poppy. "The Painted Dogs need to keep their heads as the Hot to Trots will be pressing them hard. I know this final chukka is going to be exciting." She was bobbing up and down in her chair in anticipation.

Jasper rode onto the pitch on a horse Rose did not recognise. It was all black apart from the bottom half of both back legs, which were white.

Poppy turned to her and said breathlessly, "That's Rufus's Jemima. Isn't she beautiful? I'd love to breed foals from her when she retires."

Play resumed, but it was mostly in the middle of the pitch as players and horses leaned into each other and drove other players off the line of the ball.

Suddenly, a red-shirted player galloped free of the melee and although Jasper galloped after him, the Hot to Trots scored, bringing them within one goal of the Painted Dogs.

Why had Felix left the party? And had he returned after the incident with Yaro and Jasmine? Nobody remembered seeing him, but then most of the revellers had consumed more than their fair share of alcohol.

Perhaps she should speak to Jasper or Sophia again, as they seemed to have been the only sober players. Or Dickie might remember something later, after he'd got over the stress of organising and running the Mugs Mug tournament.

On the polo pitch two players were locked in battle, galloping side by side. On the nearside was Jemima with her white back legs.

Sophia blew her whistle, stood up in her stirrups and waved her arms, but the players took no notice. Rufus cantered towards them, also blowing his whistle.

Rose watched with confusion, and then horror as play appeared to slow down and Jasper and his horse somersaulted through the air.

Jasper was thrown clear, but he curled himself into a ball as another horse and rider, unable to react in time, cantered over the top of him. There was a collective gasp as a hoof kicked Jasper's helmet.

Someone was running across the pitch. It was Rufus, and Rose watched as the players parted and she saw Jemima lying on the ground.

Without thinking, she jumped to her feet and ran as fast as she could towards the stricken horse. She heard panting beside her as Dickie joined her dash across the pitch.

Rufus was kneeling beside his horse with his arms were around her neck. She lay on her side and her whole body heaved.

Rose looked around helplessly. She needed her veterinary bag, but she'd left it at the stables.

"Mama Rose, Mama Rose," a shrill voice shouted, and she spotted a small figure moving towards her, waving an arm.

"Chumba," she gasped.

Dickie turned to her, and asked, "What?"

"Chumba's bringing my veterinary bag."

Dickie looked at the approaching figure and strode to meet him. He took the heavy bag and returned to Rose. She searched inside and withdrew her stethoscope and inserted the ear pieces.

Squatting beside the still prostrate horse she bent over it, placing the end of the stethoscope behind the girth, just below the saddle flap. The sound she heard was shallow and irregular.

The horse was winded and like a human, compression of the nerves in the stomach area had caused the diaphragm to spasm and the horse was fighting for air.

"We need to give her space and time. Rufus, you know her best. She needs to relax so her lungs can begin to work properly and draw in air."

Rose looked around for Dickie, but he was helping Jasper to his feet. Jasper's legs buckled, but Dickie held him upright as Jasper unbuckled his helmet. He shook his head.

As the strength returned to Jasper's legs and he was able to stand unsupported, one of the red-shirted players jumped off his horse, handed the reins to a teammate, and strode across to join

Dickie and Jasper. He held out a hand and said something Rose could not hear.

Jasper looked at Dickie, who nodded and shook the red-shirted man's proffered hand.

Dickie indicated to Sophia, who trotted over and bent down to listen to him. She stood up in her stirrups and blew a long, final whistle.

Holding her reins in her left hand, she drew her right hand from left to right in a flat movement, which Rose took to mean the end of the match. Those players who were still on their horses dismounted.

Rose returned to Rufus and his horse, Jemima. She listened to Jemima's lungs again with her stethoscope and was relieved to hear deeper, more regular breathing. The mare still lay with her head and neck on the ground.

Rufus wiped tears from his eyes and asked, "Is it normal for her to keep her eye closed."

Rose pursed her lips. No, it wasn't. She joined Rufus by Jemima's head and peered down at her closed eye. There was redness underneath and a yellow-coloured discharge.

"I'm sorry," said Rose, as she placed her hand on Rufus's arm. "I think her eye's been damaged, in which case she's unlikely to play again."

Rufus buried his head in his horse's neck as his whole body heaved.

CHAPTER FORTY-THREE

Rose remained on the polo pitch with Rufus Esposito and his stricken horse, Jemima, as the Painted Dogs and Hot to Trot teams led their horses back to the stables.

There was no joyous celebration. The players clapped each other on the back, or shook hands, and quietly congratulated each other.

Some spectators still stood around in groups, watching the activity on the pitch, but most had returned to the clubhouse.

Sergeant Wachira approached Rose and asked, "Is there anything we can do? Sam and Thabiti are packing away the Ol Pejeta tent, but they wanted to know if you needed any help?"

Rose looked down at the black horse, which was lying peacefully, stretched out on the ground. Rufus had carefully removed her saddle and Rose watched the regular rise and fall of Jemima's midriff with satisfaction.

Suddenly, the horse lifted her head and leaned back on her haunches. She pushed herself up into a standing position.

For a minute or so the horse just stood there, but then she shook her whole body, dropped her head and began nibbling grass.

Rufus's hands trembled as he stroked her neck and murmured, "Good girl." He picked up her reins and led her slowly back to the stables.

Rose had forgotten about Chumba, but he rushed forward as she bent down to pick up her veterinary bag.

"Thank you, Chumba, but it is heavy."

He took hold of one of the bag's handles, looked up at her, and said in a grown-up tone, "Then we both carry."

With the bag hanging between them, Rose and Chumba slowly walked across the polo pitch towards the stables. Two groundsmen wearing navy-blue overalls were removing the red and white padding from around the goal posts.

Rose was kept busy for the next ten minutes tending to minor scrapes and injuries, including the horse which had been caught up with Jemima when she fell. It had cuts on its belly and the top of a foreleg.

Otto Wakeman was holding the lead rope for a horse whose body was wet from having the sweat washed off it. His head of fair, curly hair was bent towards his syce, who was bathing the leg of his horse which had been injured earlier.

Rose approached them and Otto observed, "I can't see any reduction in the swelling yet, but we'll keep working on it. What do you recommend we do tonight?"

"I'd spread some clay on the back of the leg as it'll cool the wound and help the healing process. Then bandage it to support and immobilise the limb. Tomorrow, repeat the water cooling during the day and use clay and a bandage again in the evening. Hopefully, there'll be a noticeable reduction in the swelling."

Rose left Otto, who led the horse he was holding in the opposite direction. It was important to keep it moving to prevent any stiffness as it cooled down from the polo match.

She found Jasper Armitage leaning against the entrance poles of Jemima's stable. Rufus was inside, brushing his horse.

"How are you?" Rose asked Jasper.

"I've a splitting headache, and I've absolutely no memory of the final. Rufus has just been running through it for me."

"I saw you shake hands with the Hot to Trot team captain, before Dickie ended the match," remarked Rose.

Jasper's forehead wrinkled as he replied, "He conceded the match to us. Were we in the lead, Rufus?"

"Yes, but only by one goal."

"That was very sporting of him," admitted Jasper as he ran his hands through his sweaty hair.

Rose peered over the top of the stable and asked, "How is Jemima now?"

"Much happier," replied Rufus. "She's drunk some water and is even eating some hay. Her eye is open but there's still a yellow discharge."

"I'll give you an eye wash so you can keep it clean and I'll give her an antibiotic injection to prevent further infection. But only time will tell if she'll lose her sight, or whether she'll be able to play again."

Jasper dropped his chin to his chest and muttered, "I'm so sorry, Rufus. I know how much she means to you but I've no idea, or memory, of what happened."

Rufus began, "It was..." He stopped and bit his lip. "It was nobody's fault, just one of those things that happen in polo. An unfortunate accident. At least nobody died."

Jasper shivered and stared at his hands.

"What is it?" asked Rose kindly.

Jasper looked round at her. "I might have no memory of the final, but I do remember my discussion with Laurie Gilbert last night. Poor man, and his poor, sad wife."

Rufus stopped brushing Jemima and looked up, "Why? What's the matter with them?"

"Broken heart, I guess you'd call it, or plain old depression. Do you remember that incident at Nairobi Polo Club several years ago, when Yaro Macharia was brought down and his pony galloped off the pitch and down the track towards the Ngong Road?"

Rufus leaned against Jemima's shoulder. She turned her head towards him and he stroked her muzzle. "That was terrible. Didn't it career into a pushchair?"

"Yes, and the child never recovered, and died in hospital."

Rufus gasped, "Not Laurie Gilbert's child? Is that why his wife is … well, the way she is?"

"Sophia said she was a bright, bubbly girl before the accident and Laurie told me last night how Violet had finally enabled him to live again, after losing Sophia's mother when Sophia was young," recounted Jasper.

"Violet had been at church that morning. There's a huge one at the corner of the Ngong Road and the track leading to Jamhuri Park and the polo grounds. She was walking along the track when the horse appeared. Everyone panicked, and Violet was unable to get herself and her young boy out of the way. They were both knocked over.

"Laurie said breaking the news to her, when she woke up in hospital, was the hardest thing he's ever done. Poor man, he'd had a few beers last night and I think the alcohol was making him rather morose."

Several polo players walked past the stable, heading towards the clubhouse.

"Did Yaro give up polo after that?" asked Rufus.

Jasper frowned. "I'm not sure. I know I played against him a few weeks after the tournament and he was very cautious and wouldn't get involved in close contact play. But I think you're right, and he sold all his ponies at the end of that season."

Rose was reaching back into her memory for snippets of information about the incident. She and Craig had stopped travelling to Nairobi and only watched polo matches at the North Kenya Polo Club. Initially, the newspapers had been full of calls for justice for the young mother who'd lost her child, but the clamour had swiftly died down. She asked, "Was anyone prosecuted for causing the child's death?"

Jasper looked at her with wide eyes and replied, "Quite the opposite. You know who caused the accident and brought Yaro's horse down? Felix Kamau, and his father made sure the investigation was swiftly buried."

They stepped back as Rufus squeezed through the entrance poles of Jemima's stable.

Rufus stood up and remarked, "That's probably why Yaro's resisted sitting on a horse again for so long. When people asked him to umpire, he always refused and muttered something about falling or losing control. I guess he blamed himself."

"Come on," said Jasper. "We better go to the prize-giving. I should be exuberant after winning the Mugs Mug Cup but I feel completely drained."

As they began walking between the rows of stables, they heard a whinny. Red's head was raised and Jasper shouted across the rows of stable between him and the horse, "Good boy, I'll be back to see you later." The horse nodded his head.

Jasper remarked, "I'm surprised Laurie let Sophia play polo after what happened, but I hope her playing so well this weekend has helped cheer him up."

"You know what they say," announced Rufus. "Success is the best revenge."

CHAPTER FORTY-FOUR

Rose walked across the main polo pitch alongside Jasper Armitage and Rufus Esposito towards the clubhouse.

She asked, "Did Mr Gilbert know Sophia would be riding Excalibur this morning? Had there been any discussion about swapping horses?"

"As I understood it," replied Jasper, "Felix would ride Excalibur today, but he was considering leaving him in Timau, for Sophia to ride, and taking Red back to Nairobi. It was only a temporary measure until the end of the season. Laurie Gilbert asked me if I thought it was a good idea."

"Last night?" queried Rose.

"Yes, when we were sitting outside. Laurie admitted that Brian Ellison had recommended Excalibur for Sophia, but he'd been taken by the flashier Red. Actually, Felix was originally interested in buying Red."

Rose pondered. Had Laurie Gilbert bought Red for Sophia, knowing he was less suitable but to prevent Felix having him?

"Ah, there you are," exclaimed Dickie as he strode to meet them. "We're ready for the presentation."

Rose followed Dickie into the clubhouse. It wasn't as busy as she had expected. The players were there in their array of coloured shirts, but most of the spectators had left.

Jasmine Macharia was sitting on a chair, facing away from the fireplace. Yaro stood beside her with his hand on her shoulder and a satisfied look on his face. His nose was no longer bleeding, and he'd changed out of his umpire's shirt.

Rose joined Poppy at the far side of the room, beside the window.

Mr Gilbert stood on the other side of the window with Violet sitting on a hard-backed chair in front of him. He kept shifting his position and pulling at his collar.

Sophia entered with Jasper and Rufus. She was leaning in to hear what Rufus was saying, and she placed her hand on his arm. As Sophia passed her father, she smiled sadly at him and Violet. Mr Gilbert also looked at his wife and swayed on his feet.

Sophia grabbed his arm to support him. "Dad, are you OK?"

"I just felt a little woozy. It must be the heat. I'm fine now." Mr Gilbert gripped the back of Violet's chair with one hand and reached up and stroked his daughter's face with the other.

She gave him a quizzical look before joining her friends at the back of the room.

Dickie strode forward and stood in front of the bar. "Ladies and gentlemen," he announced, and all conversation died as everyone in the room, apart from Violet, watched him.

"First, I'd like to thank all the staff at the Timau Polo Grounds for their hard work preparing the pitches and facilities at short notice. I think you'll all agree that this is a wonderful venue and viable alternative to the current North Kenya Club pitch."

There was a smattering of applause.

"I'd also like to thank my wife and her team of caterers and bar staff who have kept us fed and watered throughout the tournament."

Behind the bar, Sam beamed and Thabiti looked down at his feet. Rose could not see Chloe or Marina.

"Before we congratulate our winning team, we have several awards to present, including two new trophies which have been generously donated this year."

Rose started. She hadn't had a chance to think about the recipient of Craig's gold tankard. Her eyes surveyed the room as she considered the individual players.

"I'd like to invite Kristopher Kamau to join me to present the first trophy." Dickie looked towards the middle of the room and nodded.

Kristopher Kamau walked forward carrying an enormous ornate silver trophy.

Dickie began, "The Felix ..."

Mr Kamau interrupted him and said, "I'm presenting this trophy in memory of my son Felix."

Rose stopped listening as Kristopher Kamau's speech moved away from his son's attributes to pontificate about his own polo career.

Violet Gilbert nibbled on arrowroot crisps and Rose observed a sheen of sweat on her husband's cheeks and forehead.

Her attention returned to Kristopher Kamau as he announced, "And the winner of the Felix Kamau Trophy for the best player is awarded jointly to Felix Kamau and Jasper Armitage."

Jasper looked at Sophia and then Rufus, who tilted his head towards the bar. Reluctantly, Jasper approached Kristopher Kamau and shook his hand. "I don't know what to say."

He stopped and looked around at the expectant faces. "Thank you. This is a great honour, and Felix was an excellent player with a bright future ahead of him. His death was tragic and for that reason I would like Mr Kamau to retain this trophy in honour of Felix."

He strode swiftly back to join his friends.

Kristopher Kamau puffed up his chest, lifted the trophy, and returned to his seat.

Dickie stepped forward and said, "Yesterday, we unveiled a portrait of our long-serving, and sorely missed committee and club member, Craig Hardie."

Dickie stopped to admire Craig's portrait before continuing, "His widow, Rose, would like to present a small trophy in his memory. Rose?" He indicated for her to join him.

Rose felt the heat rise in her cheeks as she crossed the room. Dickie leaned towards her and asked, "What would you like me to say?"

Rose glanced quickly back at the waiting crowd and replied, "If you don't mind, I think I'll speak."

Dickie nodded in appreciation.

Rose turned to the audience and took a deep breath. In a clear voice she began, "Craig valued such qualities as perseverance, hard work, honesty, kindness and graciousness. Having suffered from polio as a child, he knew better than most the training and dedication that is needed to be a polo player. But he overcame his adversity and revelled in his time as a player. Polo is a team game, so it is not always about the best player."

She stopped and smiled in Jasper's direction, and he nodded in agreement. "But about those who work together, creating the play for others who take the glory for scoring goals, or being staunch and solid in defence. I'd like to award this trophy," she lifted the gold tankard, and then placed it back on top of the bar, "to a player who I have seen grow and mature during this tournament.

"He has shown generosity in spirit and deed, and graciousness in the face of misfortune. In seeking to support others, he has acted with dignity and humility. And I very much look forward to watching his progress as a polo player over the coming years."

Rose took another deep breath. "I'd like to award the Craig Hardie Trophy to Rufus Esposito."

Rufus stood rigid and his mouth hung open. Jasper slapped him on the back and propelled him forward.

Rose smiled warmly at Rufus as he approached. She handed him the trophy and said, "Work hard, keep off the booze and you'll go far."

"Thank you," Rufus stammered and returned to his friends.

A grinning Sophie threw her arms around him and gave him a hug. As he turned back to face the bar, he wiped his eye with the back of his hand.

Dickie leaned towards Rose and whispered, "Thank you. That was very moving and Craig would be immensely proud of you."

Dickie continued to present a variety of awards to teams and individuals, including the best turned-out team, best goal, and even an award to one of the long-serving polo syces.

"And now it is time to present the final prizes. First, the runners-up, who played magnificently and made the final so exciting, the Hot to Trots."

Four red-clad men, who clearly bore a family resemblance, received their prizes. Rose glanced across at her friend Birdie Rawlinson, who was beaming.

"And finally, congratulations on a fantastic performance from our winning team, the Painted Dogs."

Those in the clubhouse who were sitting all stood to applaud the winning team. The exception was Violet Gilbert, who seemed unaware of the surrounding noise.

There were whoops and wolf-whistles as the Painted Dogs collected their prizes and held aloft the Mugs Mug trophy, which was a bronze of two polo players chasing after the ball.

As the Painted Dogs returned to the back of the room, and the clapping died down, Dickie said, "If the players would like to remain, the selectors are ready to announce their teams for next month's tour of India."

A hush fell over the room. A few people left the clubhouse, but most remained where they were.

The female selector stood in front of the bar and said, in her clipped tone, "The Men's team, representing Kenya, is Jasper Armitage, Ryan Rawlinson, Ed Jenkins and Rufus Esposito."

For the second time that afternoon, Rufus's jaw dropped in disbelief.

"And the travelling reserve is Otto Wakeman."

Otto high-fived Ed.

The female selector continued and announced the women's team. "And the travelling reserve is Sophia Gilbert."

There was a cry of joy and Rose looked around at Sophia, who was bouncing up and down on her toes. Rufus picked her up and, despite the confirmed space, swung her around.

Rose's gaze travelled back to Mr Gilbert, whose expression she couldn't read. He took the empty crisp packet that Violet waved up at him and, seemingly absentmindedly, clapped it between his hands. Rose heard it pop and, as it did, her mind cleared.

CHAPTER FORTY-FIVE

R ose strode swiftly out of the clubhouse into the courtyard. Commissioner Akida and Sergeant Wachira were sitting at a picnic bench with their heads bent over the Sergeant's notebook. They both looked up as Rose approached.

"Has the prize-giving finished?" The young sergeant asked glumly.

"It has. Have you spoken to Kristopher Kamau yet?"

Sergeant Wachira shook her head.

"We delayed speaking to him until after the prize-giving, but I suppose I'll have to face him now," said the commissioner.

"But I've still no idea what actually happened," confessed Sergeant Wachira.

"I think I have," announced Rose.

They both stared at her wide-eyed, and then the commissioner grinned. "Mama Rose solves another case."

"What's that?" demanded a loud, gruff voice.

Ms Rotich had succeeded in sneaking up to the table without any of them realising.

Commissioner Akida composed himself and replied, "Mama Rose believes she knows what happened to Felix Kamau."

Ms Rotich placed her hands on the top of the picnic table and leaned forward.

Instinctively, Rose, the commissioner and Sergeant Wachira leaned back.

"Commissioner, I shall have to reconsider your position if you continue to rely on elderly members of the public to solve your cases," the coroner said with an air of distaste.

The commissioner sat up and squared his shoulders. "I don't believe, as coroner, you have any authority over the police, or their commissioner."

Ms Rotich smirked and leaned closer to Commissioner Akida. "But I know people who do."

The commissioner set his jaw, and his eyes became cold.

"The important thing today," interrupted Sergeant Wachira, with only a slight quiver in her voice, "is to provide Mr Kamau with some answers about his son's death. I believe the police have the power to use whatever resources they see fit, including civilian consultants."

Ms Rotich's nostrils flared as she glowered at the young sergeant.

Sergeant Wachira turned to Rose and asked, "What do you need me to do?"

"Find Mr Gilbert."

As Sergeant Wachira disappeared inside the clubhouse, Ms Rotich pushed herself upright.

"Your time as commissioner is coming to an end. I know a keen, young inspector in Nairobi who'd be a perfect fit for your job, and I'll do everything in my power to see he gets it. You should have thought twice before making a fool of me." She lifted her chin and stalked away.

"Oh, dear," remarked Rose. "I was afraid she'd start throwing her weight around and trying to take control of Nanyuki's law and order. One of her mentees as commissioner is the last thing we need. You've a fight on your hands."

The commissioner's shoulders sagged. "I'm not sure I have the energy or motivation for a power struggle. I've had a good run. I'm lucky that most of the coroners I've worked with have kept out of police business, and I've been able to run things my way. Perhaps now, it's time to retire to my shamba."

Rose drew her eyebrows together. "Don't you even consider it. You've a responsibility to the community, and to Sergeant Wachira. You've taken her under your wing and persuaded her to seek promotion. How do you think she'll fare if you leave?"

The commissioner bit his lip and stood up. "Excuse me," he said, and marched across the courtyard to the clubhouse.

Sergeant Wachira passed him, escorting Mr and Mrs Gilbert. Violet sat down next to Rose without protest and toyed with her hands.

Mr Gilbert leaned against the table and asked in a tired, slightly breathless voice, "Is this really necessary? I need to sort things out for Violet."

Rose tilted her head and asked, in an even tone, "What sort of things?"

Mr Gilbert slumped onto the bench and wiped his sweating brow. "I've organised a place for her at the Cottage Hospital. Dr Farrukh has agreed to admit her to the Louise Decker Centre even though she's not physically ill. But as you can see," he reached his hand across the table towards Violet, "mentally she's like a child and needs constant care."

"But you've been managing in Nairobi, haven't you?" Rose's brow wrinkled.

"But I won't be able to care for her now, not where I'm going."

Rose noticed Mr Gilbert's lips were tinged with blue. She asked softly, "And where is that?"

Mr Gilbert smiled weakly and maintained a steady eye contact as he remarked, "I think you know. I took my revenge, but my heart is heavier than ever. I was wrong. I know that now and what I did was dreadful, unforgivable. I can't live with myself. And I can't look my daughter in the eye."

Rose leaned across the table and placed her hand over Mr Gilbert's. "This is not the only way. Sophia will be devastated. She's just entering womanhood and, without a mother, she'll rely on you for help and guidance."

Jasper, Rufus, Otto, Sophia and other members of the Kenya polo squad congregated in the entrance to the clubhouse.

They were in high spirits, talking loudly and joking about. Only Jasper remained serious as he glanced across at Rose, Mr Gilbert, and the police officers.

Sophia laughed.

Mr Gilbert glanced round and commented, "She has her friends. They'll take care of her."

"I hate to interrupt," said Sergeant Wachira, with her arms crossed, "But I think I'm missing something."

Rose looked up. "Mr Gilbert is, in his own way, admitting he was involved in Felix's death. But my current concern is his own health." She returned to Mr Gilbert and asked, "What have you taken?"

He clasped his hands together and looked down at the table. "It's too late. Even if you get me to hospital, they won't be able to help me."

"What have you taken?" repeated Sergeant Wachira in an authoritative tone.

The commissioner returned, carrying a pint of beer.

Mr Gilbert looked up and replied, "Co-proxamol and paracetamol. Together they act quickly and I only needed small amounts." He bit his blue lip. "But a beer would be nice, and help me on my way."

"I don't think so," replied Sergeant Wachira hotly, "Not if it means assisting your death."

Rose stood up and removed the glass from the commissioner's hand. "You need to keep your wits about you." She passed the beer across to Mr Gilbert, who drank appreciatively.

The commissioner stared at each of them in turn and wrinkled his nose. "Would someone mind telling me what's going on?"

CHAPTER FORTY-SIX

"Shall we all sit down?" suggested Rose to Commissioner Akida and Sergeant Wachira.

When everyone was settled, Rose said, "Mr Gilbert, you may seek your own peace, but Mr and Mrs Kamau need to know and understand what happened to their son, so they can also find closure."

Mr Gilbert sniffed and then sipped his beer. "My poor boy." He looked across at Violet and added, "Our poor boy. He was the joy of her world. I hadn't expected to have any more children, or find happiness after the death of my first wife, Sophia's mother. For many years,

I concentrated on my business and it flourished.

"Sophia's friends all rode and I was happy for her to find an activity and a social life through her ponies. I suppose it made me feel less guilty for neglecting my parental duties."

Mr Gilbert coughed, and then continued, "Violet started working for me and my life changed as she was such a bright, joyful person. She often sang to herself in the office and I would stop working just to listen to her. Sophia had been begging me to let her go to a polo match with her friends.

"I think an international team was visiting and Violet suggested she and I accompany Sophia. The match was exciting and I enjoyed the social side, speaking to people I'd done business with for years but never really got to know. When Soph asked if she could buy an old polo pony, I could hardly refuse."

Mr Gilbert smiled ruefully. "Life continued and Violet and I married and we had a baby son. Sophia said she was happy for us, even though she spent increasing amounts of time at the polo club. Sometimes Violet and I would go to matches, but usually we were content to spend a quiet Sunday at home together after Violet attended church. She joined the congregation of St. Matthew's Church, on the Ngong Road."

Mr Gilbert stared up at the clear blue sky and remarked, "But I was at the polo club on that fateful day."

"What happened?" pressed Rose.

Mr Gilbert turned to her with watery eyes and replied, "Felix cannoned into Yaro Macharia. Yaro and his horse both fell and the pony must have been spooked as it galloped off the pitch with its stirrups bouncing against the side of its saddle. And instead of trying to catch Yaro's horse, Felix called for play to resume once Yaro was back on his feet. Felix wanted to carry on as normal, but things were no longer normal for me."

Mr Gilbert paused and took a long drink of his beer. "Violet was joining me for lunch at the polo club after church. It was only a short walk to the polo club and although I wondered why she was late, I thought she must have stopped to chat to friends. Then the police turned up at the polo club and told me Violet and our son were in hospital. A loose horse had knocked them both over."

Mr Gilbert stopped and gripped the top of the table as he struggled for breath.

Sergeant Wachira bit her lip as she watched him. She said, in a contrite voice, "Don't you think we should get him to hospital?"

Rose's throat was sore, but she swallowed and replied, "Mr Gilbert is right about one thing. A doctor can't save him now. But we can help by hearing his confession."

Mr Gilbert clasped Rose's arm and whispered, "Thank you." He cleared his throat and continued, "Although the police took me straight to the hospital, my son was already dead. And when Violet woke up, I insisted I should break the news to her. But instead of screaming and wailing, she only shed silent tears. And she hasn't spoken a word since."

He leaned towards his wife and took her hands in his. As he looked at her blank face Rose thought she could hear the soft sound of humming.

"And I'll never hear her sing again." Mr Gilbert started coughing. A dry, rasping noise. After he'd stopped, he took a sip of beer and said, "After the death of my son, I spent a week being questioned by the police who kept asking why Violet was on the track with a pushchair. It was ridiculous. Hundreds of people were streaming out of church that Sunday morning.

"Witnesses said Violet tried to get out of the way but the panicked horse swerved around another group of people, straight into her. And at the end of the week, the police told me they were closing the case as they were satisfied nobody was to blame. My son had died as a result of a tragic accident."

Mr Gilbert clutched his chest as he consciously breathed in and out.

Sergeant Wachira began, "Mr Gilbert, I really think ..."

But he waved her words away. "Please, let me finish." He turned to Rose. "I was furious. You can understand that, can't you?"

Rose placed her hand on his arm and replied, "Yes, but I also know that anger and resentment can fester."

Mr Gilbert sat back. "I know, but I couldn't help it. Violet was a constant reminder of what had happened. She found my drinks cupboard and nearly drank herself to death on several occasions. I removed all alcohol from the house, but then I didn't even have that release."

He stared at his nearly empty pint of beer. "I didn't know who the player was who had caused the accident and when I asked the Nairobi Polo Club they reluctantly told me it was Felix Kamau. But they warned me against taking any further action as he was the son of the influential and wealthy politician, Kristopher Kamau. I was told that polo is a fast-paced and unpredictable game and accidents do happen. They considered that the end of the matter."

"But for you it wasn't?" suggested Rose.

"I did try to get on with life, caring for Violet and running my business. But Sophia loved polo and told me that to reach the next level, she needed more horses. She'd heard that a player was selling some, so we visited Brian Ellison's yard, outside Nakuru.

"He suggested a grey horse called Excalibur, who he said was perfect for a novice player. But the flashy Red drew my attention, and when Brian told us Felix Kamau was interested in buying him, all the old feelings flared up. I insisted we buy Red, instead of the more suitable Excalibur, as a minor victory over Felix. But it was a hollow one, as Felix then bought Excalibur."

Mr Gilbert gripped the table again and closed his eyes. He said, "When Sophia told me she had a place in a team for this weekend's tournament, I felt drawn to attend. I didn't intend to harm Felix, at least I don't think I did."

Mr Gilbert stopped and Rose exchanged looks with the commissioner and Sergeant Wachira.

Rose asked quietly, "So what happened?"

Mr Gilbert opened his eyes but stared at the table. "Before the party, I promised myself I would try to enjoy the evening and support Sophia. She was so happy and I was amazed at how well she played, even though some of her teammates insisted on shouting at her.

"Jasper Armitage was really welcoming, and I relaxed and had a few drinks. I suppose I could feel the tension rising around me and it centred on Felix. Sophia insisted he was a pleasant young man and yet he was still causing trouble. I heard him tell someone he was going to check on his horses. I told Jasper I needed some air, or something like that, and I followed Felix, but realised I wasn't the only one."

Sophia walked towards the table, but Commissioner Akida stood up and intercepted her. Rose heard him say, "Your father is just helping us with our enquiries. You'll be able to speak to him shortly."

Sophia gave her father an anxious look before rejoining her friends. There was a pop as one of them opened a bottle of champagne.

Mr Gilbert jumped. He struggled for breath and then rasped, "Rufus Esposito was very drunk and started shouting about Felix being spoilt and having anything he wanted. That he had no idea what it was like for everyone else. The surrounding horses started to stamp their feet and walk around their stables. Rufus tried to hit Felix, but he fell over.

"A young boy ran to help him and supported him as they staggered towards the gate leading to Wild Dog Estate. I was about to confront Felix myself when Jasmine Macharia tottered into view and threw herself at him. It wasn't long before her husband arrived and he started shouting at Felix. He also tried to hit Felix but hurt himself when Felix dodged his punch. Jasmine led her husband away, but now the horses were really upset.

"Felix began walking along the rows of stables, talking to the horses to calm them down. I met him outside the stables where Sophia's horses were. Red was stamping his feet, tossing his head and spinning round inside his stable. I said I was worried about him and Felix told me not to be, and he'd settle him.

"Felix climbed between the two entrance poles into the stable but, despite whispering to the horse and stroking its neck, Red was still very upset. He kept kicking out with his back legs. I'm not sure why I did it, but I found one of Violet's empty crisp packets in my pocket. I blew into it and clapped it between my hands. It made a bang, almost like a gunshot in the still air.

"The surrounding horses panicked. I looked up just as Red turned and kicked out with both back legs and caught Felix in the chest, propelling him back against the metal bars of the stable."

Mr Gilbert stopped and coughed. He clutched his chest and looked up at Rose. Pain was etched across his face. "I should have done something. Let Red out of his stable so he couldn't cause any more harm. Called for help. Maybe I would have done if Soph hadn't lost her phone. But I walked away and left Felix lying there.

"And that's why I can't live with myself. I'm a coward and a murderer. I'm worse than Felix. I caused the incident which led to his death and I didn't try to save him."

Rose reached into her trouser pocket and removed an empty folded packet of arrowroot crisps which she'd picked up outside Red's stable this morning, when they'd found Felix's body.

CHAPTER FORTY-SEVEN

M r Gilbert gripped the edge of the picnic table and half stood, but his body was racked with coughs and he gasped for air.

Sophia detached herself from her friends and ran across the courtyard crying, "Dad, what's wrong?"

Mr Gilbert sank back onto the bench and muttered, "Soph, please forgive me."

"Forgive you for what?"

"Everything, and please take care of Violet for me. She never deserved any of this."

Mr Gilbert's breathing was shallow, and he made a rasping noise.

Rose whispered, "Is there anything I can do?"

Mr Gilbert tried to shake his head, but stopped and swayed.

Sophia sat down next to her father and wrapped an arm around him. In a high-pitched voice, she asked, "What's wrong? Why aren't you helping him?"

Rose's voice was gentle as she replied, "There's nothing I can do. Your father has decided to end his pain. He's taken an overdose and shortly he'll drift away."

"Overdose? Of what? We need to get him to hospital."

She tried to stand and drag her father upright, but he slumped forward across the table. "Help me!" screamed Sophia.

Conversations died as people watched and Jasper and Rufus ran towards Sophia.

Rose felt Mr Gilbert's pulse. It was very faint. "It's time to say goodbye." Rose tried to maintain a steady voice. "Tell him you love him."

Rose turned her head and wiped a tear from her eye as Sophia shook her father and pleaded with him, "Don't go. Don't die. I need you."

Commissioner Akida had listened to the entire exchange with a passive look on his face. He placed a hand on Rose's shoulder and as she looked up he asked, in a matter-of-fact tone, "Please, can you check Mr Gilbert."

Rose felt a knot in her stomach as she reached for Mr Gilbert's wrist. There was no pulse. She gulped and pronounced, "He's dead."

The commissioner took charge of the situation. "Sergeant Wachira, please contact the Cottage Hospital and ask them to collect Mr Gilbert's body."

"What about Mrs Gilbert?" asked the young sergeant with a shaky voice.

Jasper stepped forward and said, "I'll take her and Sophia to the hospital."

"I don't understand. What's happening?" wailed Sophia.

"I'll go with them." Rufus put his arm around Sophia and led her away. Jasper guided Violet after them.

Rose watched them leave with an aching heart. The commissioner removed his cap and stood beside her as he, too, watched the forlorn party.

Ms Rotich bustled over and announced, "Just what is going on?"

Sergeant Wachira appeared with a white tablecloth which she draped over Mr Gilbert's body.

Ms Rotich's hand flew to her mouth. She staggered to the clubhouse wall and was sick.

Kristopher Kamau was standing at the entrance to the clubhouse. Commissioner Akida strode across and ushered him back inside.

Marina appeared and silently handed Rose a cup of tea. As Rose sipped the sugary liquid, she realised there was nothing sweet about revenge. The tea suddenly tasted bitter and she placed her cup on the table, next to the inert form of Mr Gilbert.

CHAPTER FORTY-EIGHT

Rose's hands still shook as she drove her battered, red Land Rover Defender home to Nanyuki. She was used to death and had lost her beloved Craig only two months earlier.

But needless death? Those dying before their naturally allotted time? Somehow, that was different.

Rose had left Chumba at the Timau Polo Grounds to take care of Felix's ponies, but he couldn't stay indefinitely, as school started soon. But that was a problem for next week.

She parked her car in the dilapidated wooden garage, but rather than entering the house, she wandered down to the stables.

There was a yap and a patter of paws as Potto, her black-and-tan terrier raced past, stopped to look at her and then bounded down the path.

Izzy, her black and white cat, was lying on a piece of tarpaulin outside the lean-to where Rose kept her dried herbs. She stretched lazily as Rose approached.

Whoosh, her horse, and his pony companion, Bahati, were grazing peacefully in the small field alongside her cow, Bette. Rose leant against the post-and-rail fence and watched them. The normality and simplicity of the scene soothed and comforted her.

She felt a vibration in her pocket and reached for her phone.

"Sorry to disturb you," said the commissioner when she answered the call. "Mr Kamau would like us to join him and his wife for lunch at the Mount Kenya Resort and Spa tomorrow. I know he'll want more details about Felix's death, so do you feel up to it?"

Whoosh lifted his head and moved forward several paces before nibbling at a fresh patch of grass. Rose thought of Mrs Kamau and wondered how she was coping with the loss of her son.

"I'll come," replied Rose.

On Monday morning, Rose waved a thank you to the security guard as he lifted the barrier and allowed her to enter the Mount Kenya Resort and Spa. She had arrived early so that she could check on the resort's horses and guard dogs.

She parked in the overflow car park, rather than beside the hotel's entrance, and took the path which ran in front of the hotel, past the swimming pool.

It was mid-morning and several guests were lying on sun loungers or enjoying drinks under the shade of canvas umbrellas. Only two guests were brave enough to swim in the resort's chilly pool.

Rose reached the stables and began to examine the face and mouth of the horse in the first stable. She patted its neck, satisfied that the sores, from an ill-fitting bridle, had healed.

There was still a hairless patch under its tummy where the girth had rubbed, so she'd instruct the syce to apply the ointment she'd given him for such wounds on her last visit. She also needed to check he was regularly washing the horse's girth.

As she entered the next stable, a serene voice asked, "Are you Mama Rose? Did you discover what had happened to my son, Felix?"

Rose turned around slowly, composing herself before facing Mrs Kamau.

"I am, and I suppose I did. I'm very sorry for your loss. How are you?"

The horse moved towards the open stable door, but Mrs Kamau stepped forward, to prevent it from escaping, and stroked its muzzle.

"Empty," replied Mrs Kamau. "I don't think I have any tears left. Felix may have been competitive on the polo pitch, but he was a fair and honest boy. Did I overhear my husband correctly? Was Felix's death connected with that terrible incident in Nairobi, where a woman and her young child were knocked down and the child died?"

Rose ran her hand down the horse's leg and replied, "It appears so."

"Felix begged his father to allow him to speak to the police, but Kristopher refused. As usual, my husband dealt with the matter in his own way. He assured Felix he was not to blame and that it was an accident, and he sent him to Australia for six months to improve his polo skills."

Rose stood up and stretched her back. She felt drained by the events of the weekend. She turned to Mrs Kamau and asked, "So Felix may not have realised the child was Sophia's half-brother?"

Mrs Kamau shook her head sadly. "He had no idea."

Rose and Mrs Kamau joined Commissioner Akida and Kristopher Kamau on the terrace outside the main hotel dining room.

The portly manager, Mr Bundi, grasped Rose's hand in greeting and exclaimed, "Mama Rose, it's good to see you again, and in such esteemed company." He beamed at Mrs Kamau.

When Rose and Mrs Kamau were settled at the table, with glasses of champagne, Mr Kamau turned to Rose and asked, "Please, can you explain exactly what happened to my son, and why?"

Rose repeated the story Mr Gilbert had told her. She struggled to keep the emotion from her voice, especially when she repeated the events which led to the death of Mr Gilbert's young son.

When she had finished, Mrs Kamau dabbed her eyes with a white, lace-edged handkerchief. She reached over and touched Rose's arm, and murmured, "Thank you."

Mr Kamau puffed out his chest and turned to Commissioner Akida. "Is that it? Is there nothing more you can do?"

"I'm afraid not," replied the commissioner in a level voice. "Some would say justice has been served."

Rose glanced at him and wondered exactly what he meant. And justice for whom? The child was dead. So were Felix and Mr Gilbert, and Violet would live the rest of her life in a care home. She looked down at her hands.

Mrs Kamau broke the silence. "We had a visit this morning from two of Felix's friends and fellow polo players."

Mr Kamau muttered under his breath.

His wife gave him a cynical look and continued. "One of them was Sophia Gilbert, so my husband refused to meet them, and she was accompanied by that dark-featured player, Rufus Esposito. They were asking about the future of Felix's polo ponies."

"Sell them," interrupted her husband.

Mrs Kamau ignored him and continued, "They suggested pooling Felix's ponies with their own, and Jasper Armitage's whilst he's playing in the UK, to create a large polo yard, based in Timau. They'd like to give inexpensive, and even free, polo lessons to young and novice players, and provide horses for those who cannot afford their own."

Mr Kamau announced, "Come on, Commissioner, let's see what's for lunch."

Mrs Kamau continued, "I told them it was an excellent idea, and I gave them my blessing."

Her husband stalked away.

Mrs Kamau folded her handkerchief and returned it to her bag. "It's time to put an end to this sorry affair. There's no point holding onto grievances and anyway, Sophia had nothing to do with her father's actions."

Mrs Kamau turned to Rose and confided, "And I've agreed to invest and support their venture. Felix enjoyed helping young, enthusiastic players and I'm sure he would have approved."

"I'm sure he would," agreed Rose. "And you're right, it is time for everyone to move on."

They stood and entered the restaurant.

CHAPTER FORTY-NINE

Rose returned to the Timau Polo Grounds on Tuesday morning to check on her equine patients and collect Chumba and his meagre belongings.

She passed a red-faced Otto Wakeman who was jogging down the track leading away from the polo ground.

The first person she met at the stables was Poppy, who was removing the entrance poles to Jemima's stable. "Come along," she instructed the horse and led it out.

She turned and spotted Rose. "Hello, Rose. Good timing. Would you mind checking Jemima over before I lead her across to my house?"

Rose deposited her veterinary bag on the ground and approached the attractive black horse. She peered at Jemima's eye, which was no longer oozing yellow liquid, and said, "I don't know if she's lost any, part, or all of her sight. Just be careful when approaching her from this side, in case she has trouble seeing you."

Poppy looked around the stable area. "Poor Dickie, he thought the tournament was going to be a success after the first day, but with the deaths and thieves, and Jasper's terrible fall in the final, it didn't end well. At least we don't need to use the Timau Polo Grounds again this season."

"Oh, why's that?"

"We can return to the North Kenya Polo Club pitch as the African wild dogs have moved on."

"With their young cubs?"

Poppy nodded. "A local farmer thought they were hunting his sheep so he retaliated and shot one of them."

Rufus Esposito appeared around the corner of the stable block. He walked up to Jemima and draped an arm around her neck. "Now you behave for Mrs Chambers, and if you're a good girl, she might even let you have babies."

Jemima's large ears flicked back and forth as if she was listening.

Rufus removed his arm and turned to Poppy. "Thank you for taking her. She deserves a loving home and I think she'll be quiet to ride if you want to hack her out."

"I'd better go," announced Poppy. "Rose, I'll see you in town later this week." She led Jemima away.

Rufus picked up Rose's veterinary bag and asked, "Can you check on Trigger and Boadicea?"

"Is Jasper here?"

"No, he was called to the UK to play for the Berkshire Mad Hatters. One of the team had a fall at the weekend and broke his arm. I'm not sure Jasper will join us in India now, but Otto has started training. He says he needs to improve his fitness and has started running."

Rufus scratched his stubbled chin.

Rose checked Trigger, Jasper's palomino horse first. She ran her hand down his back legs. "I can't feel any heat, but I don't think he should return to work just yet."

Rufus, who was leaning against the entrance poles, replied, "Don't worry. Jasper has asked us to turn him and Boadicea out in the field and give them a break until next season. I'm waiting for Soph now and then we'll lead them both to her plot on Wild Dog Estate. They can rest there but we'll still play Biscuit and Storm, and your young boy, Chumba, is keen to have a go."

"He has school, but I'm sure he can help out at weekends, and you can give him some lessons."

"We've given him one of Felix's old polo sticks and some balls to practise with at home." Rufus stepped back as Rose climbed through the entrance bars and out of the stable.

"I'm not sure what Bahati would think of that. He's still very nervous."

Rufus chuckled. "He doesn't need to ride. He can sit astride a fence and practice his polo swings."

"Just as long as he doesn't break anything," responded Rose dubiously.

Rufus attached a head collar to Boadicea and led her out of her stable.

Rose bent down to examine the horse's knee, which was still puffy. "You'll need to keep an eye on this and keep applying the cold water treatment. But at least in the field she'll wander around, which should keep the swelling down."

Sophia approached them. She looked even thinner, and her face was grey with large bags under her eyes.

"How are you?" Rose asked.

Sophia leant against a stable and confessed, "Not great. I'm used to being on my own and looking after myself, but I keep expecting a call from Dad, just to check how I'm getting on, or to tell me a delivery of timber's arriving for the house. I suppose I should try to complete it, for him."

"And what about Violet?" Rose enquired in a gentle voice.

Sophia wrinkled her mouth. "I'm not sure she realises or understands that Dad is … dead." She gulped. "But she seems content in her own world, and being looked after by the staff at the Cottage Hospital. I visited her, to check she'd settled in, but she didn't recognise me." Sophia rubbed her eyes.

Rufus asked, "Shall we move these horses then?"

Sophia straightened up. "Of course. And then we need to rearrange stabling so our horses, Felix's, and Biscuit and Storm are in the same block."

Rose was about to mention their new venture and their backer, Mrs Kamau, but she thought now was not the time.

Sophia led Trigger out of his stables, and she and Rufus slowly led their horses away.

Rose checked Otto's injured horse. The back of its front leg was still bowed, so she gave it another injection of the anti-inflammatory drug, Phenylbutazone.

When she'd finished, she called, "Chumba!"

He appeared around the corner carrying a bundle of bedding and balancing his new polo stick which wobbled precariously on top.

He wore a polo helmet and on his back was a very full, old canvas bag. He dropped everything to the ground and said, "I still have other bags and bucket."

He dashed off and returned carrying two plastic shopping bags in one hand and a black bucket, filled with white polo balls, brushes and pieces of tack, in the other.

"Where did you get all these from?" asked Rose, as she surveyed the items on the ground.

"Master Rufus sorted out Felix and Jasper's polo gear and gave me some old things." Chumba beamed with pride. "He said I do a good job and give me five thousand shillings. He said Felix's Mum give him to give to me. Nice lady. Like Felix."

Chumba's face fell. "Poor Mr Felix. I like working for him."

"But Rufus said you can come and help him and Sophia, and they'll give you polo lessons."

Chumba brightened and enthused, "And look," he picked up the polo stick, "they give me this to practise with."

"You'll need to work hard. But now it's time to go home."

CHAPTER FIFTY

O n Thursday morning Rose stepped through the metal arch into the courtyard outside Dormans coffee shop.

She spotted Thabiti leaning over a table and discussing something with Hellen Newton, the manager of Nanyuki's branch of Jengo Real Estate.

As Rose approached them, Thabiti pointed at something on a large sheet of paper which was spread across the table, and said, "And the three-phase electricity will come in here to power the coffee machine."

Hellen looked up and said, "Habari, Mama Rose."

Rose realised the paper was another architect's plan.

"We've made some changes to the refurbishment of the building on Dr Emma's new plot," explained Thabiti.

"We're adding some partition walls here, and here," he pointed at the drawing, "to create an extra examination room and a holding area for animals before they're seen by a vet. We're also constructing a kennels area at the back so owners can drop their dogs off for treatment, and some may need to stay overnight."

Rose put her glasses on and studied the plan. She touched it with her finger and asked, "What's this area?"

"That's a covered patio for the cafe. It wraps around the front corner of the building. Most of the space will be for tables and chairs but I'd like to build a raised platform, surrounded by an oversized shelf with power points under it, so people can sit and drink coffee or eat, but still work on their laptops."

Rose stood upright and asked, "And what does Dr Emma think?"

"She's delighted," beamed Thabiti.

Hellen Newton said, "I think she's relieved that Thabiti has taken responsibility for the building work. The proposals for the cafe and deli will enhance the value of that space and she'll get a shiny new veterinary facility."

Hellen turned back to Thabiti and said, "Let me know if you want to discuss anything else." She picked up her bag and car keys and added, "Better dash, I'm late for an appointment."

Chloe and Marina passed Hellen as they walked into the courtyard. They strode across to join Rose and Thabiti.

"Oh, are these the amended plans?" exclaimed Chloe.

Marina studied the drawing and asked, "The outside area looks rather small. Are you sure we'll have enough room?"

Thabiti tapped the plan and replied nervously, "We agreed the patio would come out six metres. I think the scale of the plan is deceptive."

"Of course there'll be enough room," enthused Chloe. "And if we get really busy, we can add individual tables and umbrellas, just like here." She indicated to the picnic-style tables, shaded by canvas umbrellas, in the courtyard around them.

Marina smiled hesitantly. "What do I know about building work?" She sat down.

Thabiti rolled up the plan. "But you know about cooking. The food at the polo club was delicious."

"Thank you." Marina's smile was warmer. "But it was hard work. And next time we won't have your friend Dotty to help us." She looked across at Chloe.

Chloe tilted her head to the right. "Dotty's nice, but she's completely ruled by Al. I hope she gets a chance to make something of her life and not just follow her husband around, hosting military dinner parties."

"Those scotch eggs were a winner," declared Thabiti. "Will you make them for the deli?"

"Possibly, and maybe sausage rolls and some pies," replied Marina. "We've so many ideas, haven't we?" She turned to Chloe.

"Yes, but first you and Pearl have your trip to India. As well as clothes, see what knik-knaks and present-type gifts you can find. It would be lovely to offer the people of Nanyuki something more than carved wooden animals and photo frames, or soapstone ornaments."

Marina looked up at Rose, who was still standing, and asked, "And what about you? What are you plans for September?"

Rose replied, "To have a quiet time, without any dead bodies."

Were you as surprised as Rose when Chloe's timid houseguest, Dotty Sayers, rebuked a gentleman for taking too much lunch?

Rose was right, there is more to Dotty than meets the eye, but after many years being dominated by her father and her husband she's become used to doing as she's told.

So what would happen to Dotty if her husband was killed on a military operation? And how would she react when she takes a temporary job in an antiques centre, and a body is discovered in a giant grandfather clock?

Hour is Come is the FREE prequel to the Dotty L. Sayers Antique Mysteries and will be available to subscribers of my newsletter first.

If you're not already on my mailing list sign up for Hour is Come at,

www.bit.ly/SignUpHourIsCome

For more information visit VictoriaTait.com